U0011011

全民英檢初級

聽力測驗

曾利娟◎著

晨星出版

Melody 的魔力教學

外籍人士推薦　Mark Heffner

To those preparing to take the General English Proficiency Test (GEPT),

It is with joy that I am able to highly recommend, to the students and teachers who are facing GEPT, this preparatory practice test book. This preparatory practice exam book is an excellent resource for you in the near future.

As I have previewed the material myself recently, I was impressed with its detailed understanding of key testing skills and foundational linguistic necessities.

給正在準備參加全民英檢的同學們：

我很高興能夠向正在準備全民英檢的老師和學生們鄭重推薦這本考試準備書籍。這本考試用書對你們來說將會是不可多得的資源。

我已先拜讀了這本教材，裡面有關於重要考試技巧和語言根基要點的細節講解讓我十分佩服。

我發現這裡面的10次模擬試題是經過作者仔細和完整的建構，讓讀者有充分及萬全的準備，來通過全民英檢。這本書完全是依照全民英檢聽

I found the 10 mock test exams to be carefully thought through and clearly constructed for the purpose of allowing adequate and excellent preparation to pass GEPT. The book is designed with the same layout and test structure as the listening test of GEPT thus laying a good preparatory foundation for the test-taker. The similarity of the book with the actual test will help give confidence to you. The mock tests in the book and CD highlight key vocabulary and grammatical phrases very likely to be on the tests or similar to the ones on the test.

Regardless of whether one decides to actually take the test, the book and CD is an excellent resource packet for language improvement for the non-native speaker of English. This curriculum, if studied and used wisely, will aid one throughout one's life in the area of English language proficiency.

The CD combined with the exam preparation book will provide adequate and thorough preparation. You should find that

力測驗的內容和考試架構來設計，因此可以為參加考試者奠定很好的基礎。書中的內容和實際的考試極為相似，因此可以幫助學生增強信心。書和CD中的模擬試題所特別強調的關鍵字和文法片語，即可能出現在正式試題中。

不管是否決定要參加考試，對於英語非本國語言的人來說，如果想增進語言的能力，本書和CD亦為絕佳的參考書。如果認真的跟著裡面的課程來學習，將會幫助你在英文的領域中突飛猛進。

此書與CD的搭配，可以提供學生合適且完整的練習。你會發現你的考試技巧越來越進步，並且越來越有信心在考試當

your test taking ability will improve and gain confidence to experience success on test day. It will be also a very useful tool for you to learn the vocabulary, phrases, and scenarios that happen frequently in daily conversation.

The preparatory testing book will help give you an accurate picture of where you are at in regards to the linguistic skills necessary to pass the English exam. I look forward with great anticipation to see how this 10-test book will be beneficial to exam-takers in Taiwan in your quest to better your own individual English language ability and prepare for the GEPT.

I believe this book also will be a very useful tool for Taiwan society as a whole, as it strives to make English language acquisition a top academic, business and educational priority in this new century!

Sincerely,

Mark Heffner

天可以拿到好成績。這本書也是你學習日常對話中常出現的單字、片語和句子的實用工具書。

這本考試準備書籍會幫助你更精確的了解,自己在通過英文測驗所需的語言技巧上具備了多少能力。我非常期待見到這10回測驗能夠成為台灣參加考試者的幫助,不管是提昇個人英文能力或是準備考試,這本書都會是非常大的幫助。

我相信這本書對台灣整體社會來說也將會是很有用的工具書,因它致力於在新世紀中使英語學習在學術、商業和教育的領域裡佔舉足輕重的地位!

Mark Heffner 敬上

Melody 的魔力教學

外籍人士推薦　Laura Titus Heffner

I highly recommend this preparatory practice test book for those preparing to take the GEPT (General English Proficiency Test). This book has been expertly researched and is an invaluable resource for those preparing to take the GEPT listening test in the near future.

Of particular benefit to test-takers are the 10 practice tests. In both content and structure, these tests are so similar to the actual exam that after practicing them you

我向正在準備全民英檢的人極力推薦這本考試練習教材。這本書的著作經過專業的研究，對於即將要參加全民英檢聽力考試的人來說，是非常珍貴的資源。

這本書對於要考試的人來說，最特殊的優點在於十回練習的考試題目，這些考試題目在內容和結構上都和真正的考試非常相似。在練習完這些題目後，你就可以充滿信心的去應試了。

另一個優點在於關鍵字的強調，這幫助學生更容易了解聽力的內容。你只要專注

can proceed to exam day with confidence.

Another benefit is the key words highlighted to make listening much easier to comprehend. You can only focus on a couple of words to catch the overall meaning.

The last benefit, but not least, is a lot of tips on how to solve a number of listening problems.

This test is highly regarded by the Taiwan government and a lot of schools. Having the GEPT certificate will be a great benefit in one's current career as well as in the pursuit of a new job or job promotion. But, even if one should decide to not actually take the test, the book and CD is an excellent resource for language improvement for non-native English speakers. This curriculum can be a useful tool throughout one's life not only in the area test preparation, but in English language proficiency.

在幾個字上就可以理解整個句子／對話的意思。

最後，但也是很重要的優點在於，書裡有許多的小技巧，告訴你如何解決一些聽力測驗上的問題。

現今台灣政府和許多的學校機構都非常重視全民英檢，擁有全民英檢的證照對於個人當前的工作、新工作的找尋或是在職場上的晉升都有非常大的助益。然而，即使決定不去參加考試，這本書及CD對於英語非本國語言的人來說，仍是提升語言能力很棒的資源。裡面的課程將是生活中的實用教材，不只是對考試的準備上有幫助，對個人英語專業能力的提升來說也是同樣有極大的益處。

I anticipate great results for those who properly use and study this preparatory book and CD!

Laura Titus Heffner

我相信所有正確使用這本書籍和CD來學習的人都會有優越的成效！

Laura Titus Heffner

英檢聽力得分技巧大解析

By Melody

第一部分：看圖辨義

第一部分看圖辨義是「只有圖片沒有文字」的測驗，是根據你所看到的圖及聽到的Ａ、Ｂ、Ｃ三個選項去選一個與圖片吻合的答案。

得分關鍵：快速分析圖片架構有助於預測題目方向。

在完全沒有文字的情況下，必須先瀏覽圖片內容並分析圖片架構，再去猜想可能會聽到什麼。

例如：圖中有人、貓與狗，即可推測題目可能是：場景為何？事件？貓狗數量？人與貓狗的活動或位置……等。

另要你特別注意，有時一張圖片會出現兩個題目，在作答時務必注意題號。可藉由本書的十回聽力測驗，訓練自己在CD播放前快速瀏覽圖片，且不要因前一題聽不懂而影響下一題瀏覽圖片的動作。若能充分掌握時間並做到圖片的預覽與分析，就能在聽力測驗取得分數。

第二部分：問答

本單元是播放甲方說的一句話，測驗乙方（考生）應如何回應，並於Ａ、Ｂ、Ｃ三選項中選出最適合的答案。

得分關鍵：閱讀能力——因為閱讀速度太慢或無法瞭解選項內容，而導致失分。

基本上，本單元除測驗聽力外，因必須快速瞭解選項內容，所以也著重於基本的閱讀能力。雖然語言學習的四種技能（聽、說、讀、寫）可以分開測驗，但在學習過程中，四種技能的關係卻是密不可分且能同時培養，如在「說」的同時也訓練聽力，在閱讀時可以學習寫作技巧。

本單元重點在於：瞭解選項間的差異。例如：選項有著不同的時態

時，則須注意問話中的時態；又或者選項 A 是場所、B 是動作、C 是情緒，則可在快速閱讀後推測題目方向並選出正確答案。

根據筆者多年的教學經驗，就算只有幾秒鐘，考生仍應確實瀏覽考題，否則要同時兼顧「聽」並分析選項內容，再選出合適答案是非常困難的。所以應在這十回的測驗題中，養成預留時間瀏覽題目的習慣。最常見的考試失常狀況，便是多數考生心情緊張且未經訓練，即因前幾題聽不懂，又沒有預留時間閱讀下一題，便在要兼顧聽與閱讀的壓力下，導致應得分的題目卻無法正確作答。

第三部分：簡短對話

本單元是三個部分中最困難的，因聽力內容較長。兩人（通常是一男一女）對話內容約有 4-6 句，並在對話後提出問題，要求從 A、B、C 三選項中，選出最適合的答案。

得分關鍵：即使對話內容不全懂也能得分，但最後一句對話是考題，一定要聽懂。

請試著在 CD 中聽到筆者於解答中為考生標示的關鍵字，你將會發現只要聽得懂關鍵字就可以得分。還可試著從兩人談話的語調推測所在的場景或兩人間的關係，常見問題是問兩人關係為何。如：夫妻、師生、朋友、老闆與職員、還是客戶與店員。根據財團法人語言中心對外發佈的「全民英檢初級的考試範圍是生活基本用語」與其信度可知，測驗內容將不會出現學術性及專業性用詞，而是以旅遊、購物、問候語、電話應對禮儀、餐廳基本等對話為主。

註：信度係指告知考試的內容為何，實際上考試的內容與告知的吻合度。

編註：本書以 MP3 光碟播出，而並非以錄音帶播出，但為配合實際考試狀況故說明文的內容與全民英檢幾乎一致。

目錄
CONTENTS

本測驗分三部份，全部都是單選題，共30題，作答時間約20分鐘。作答說明為中文，印在試題冊上並經由錄音播出。

第一部分：看圖辨義

共10題，每題請聽錄音播出題目和三個英文句子之後，選出與所看到的圖畫最相符的答案。每題只播出一遍。

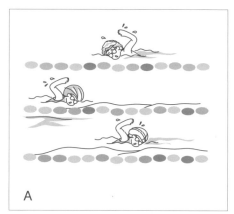

A

B

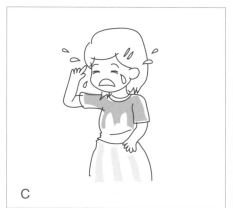

C

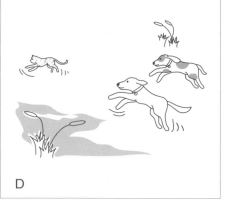

D

E

F

G

H

考題請翻下一頁 ▶

第二部分：問答

共10題，每題請聽錄音播出的英文句子，再從試題冊上三個回答中，選出一個最適合的答案。每題只播出一遍。

11. A. I am at home.
    B. I am going to the park.
    C. I went to school.

12. A. By practicing a lot.
    B. Long time no see.
    C. Decide where to go.

13. A. This is the ladies' room.
    B. Who is your sister?
    C. She is my best friend, Lily.

14. A. Really, when?
    B. Who did you get married to?
    C. I am sorry to hear that.

15. A. There are many kinds of books.
    B. They are in the backyard.
    C. Call me later.

16. A. It is made in Taiwan.
    B. My father told me.

C. It cost me only $500.

17. A. I am telling you the truth.

    B. I am not telling a lie.

    C. I will call her back soon. Thanks!

18. A. I will call 119.

    B. Oh, no! I hate rainy days.

    C. It comes from the sky.

19. A. By car.

    B. We took a trip to Hualian.

    C. July 16th.

20. A. It is 500 miles.

    B. Twice a year.

    C. Around 30 minutes.

第三部份：簡短對話

    共10題，每題請聽錄音播出一段對話和一個相關的問題後，再從試題冊上三個選項中，選出一個最適合的答案。每段對話和問題播出<u>兩遍</u>。

21. A. The woman did not know Kathy.

    B. The man has seen Kathy recently.

    C. Neither of them has seen Kathy recently.

22. A. He is going to buy three pieces of cheese.

    B. He is taking a picture of the woman.

    C. He makes the woman eat cheese.

23. A. He is going to get married.

    B. He is going to pass the exam.

    C. He is going to graduate.

24. A. A train station.

    B. A gas station.

    C. A post office.

25. A. The man's mom.

    B. The woman's mom.

    C. The woman who is talking.

26. A. He is going abroad.

    B. He wants to share the bill.

    C. He doesn't want to pay for the bill.

27. A. He is a doctor.

    B. He is a waiter.

    C. He is a police man.

28. A. She is sleeping.

    B. She is waking up the man.

C. She is going to school.

29. A. The man's.
    B. Maria's.
    C. Nancy's.

30. A. She is a patient.
    B. She is a nurse.
    C. She is a teacher.

第一部分：看圖辨義聽力詳述解答

(B) 1. For question 1, please look at picture A.
Where are they?
A. They are boys.
B. They are in a swimming pool.
C. They are drinking water in a river.

(B) 2. For question 2, please look at picture A again.
How many people are swimming?
A. Only one man is swimming.
B. Three people are swimming.
C. Nobody is swimming.

(C) 3. For question 3, please look at picture B.
Where is the old man sitting?
A. He is sitting on the side.
B. He is sitting between the boy and the girl.
C. He is sitting between the two boys.

(B) 4. For question 4, please look at picture C.
How is the girl feeling?
A. She looks very excited.
B. She looks very sad.
C. She looks very proud.

（C） 5. For question 5, please look at picture D.

What is happening here?

A. Two cats are running after a dog.

B. A dog is running after two cats.

C. Two dogs are running after a cat.

（C） 6. For question 6, please look at picture E.

Who is holding a baby?

A. The old woman is.

B. The young girl is.

C. The man is.

【英文常識】hold 這個字表示擁抱、握住，hold 最常見的片
語是 hold on。

hold on 表示稍等一下或是請人不要掛掉電話。這個片
語最早期是來自於以前的電話如果不要掛掉時，就一定
要握住--hold，且要保持開機的狀況，而 on 即表示電源
開啓的狀態，所以 hold on 可表示電話不要掛掉且沿用
到現在，即使不是使用電話對談，我們還是可以用 hold
on 來表示稍等或稍候。

（A） 7. For question 7, please look at picture F.

Who is standing at the table?

A. A waitress.

B. A customer.

C. A couple.

（C） 8. For question 8, please look at picture G.

What is the weather like?

A. It is pretty hot.

B. It is summer.

C. It is cold.

【句型】What is the weather like?= How is the weather?

（C） 9. For question 9, please look at picture H.

Where are they?

A. They are in the library.

B. They are in the bank.

C. They are on the beach.

（C） 10. For question 10, please look at picture H again.

What are they doing?

A. They are playing volleyball.

B. They are playing with dolls.

C. They are playing in the sand.

【單字】volleyball (n.) 排球

第二部分：問答聽力詳述解答

（B） 11. Where are you going?

    A. I am at home.

    B. I am going to the park.

    C. I went to school.

（A） 12. Amazing! How can you do it?

    A. By practicing a lot.

    B. Long time no see.

    C. Decide where to go.

（C） 13. Who is the pretty young lady?

    A. This is the ladies' room.

    B. Who is your sister?

    C. She is my best friend, Lily.

（A） 14. I am going to get married.

    A. Really, when?

    B. Who did you get married to?

    C. I am sorry to hear that.

（B） 15. Where are the kids?

    A. There are many kinds of books.

    B. They are in the backyard.

    C. Call me later.

(C) 16. How much did you spend on the bike?

　　　A. It is made in Taiwan.

　　　B. My father told me.

　　　C. It cost me only $500.

(C) 17. Your mother just called.

　　　A. I am telling you the truth.

　　　B. I am not telling a lie.

　　　C. I will call her back soon. Thanks!

(B) 18. It is going to rain tomorrow.

　　　A. I will call 119.

　　　B. Oh, no! I hate rainy days.

　　　C. It comes from the sky.

(B) 19. Where did you go on vacation last month?

　　　A. By car.

　　　B. We took a trip to Hualian.

　　　C. July 16th.

【片語】take a trip to... = 去……旅行

(C) 20. How long have you waited?

　　　A. It is 500 miles.

　　　B. Twice a year.

C. Around 30 minutes.

第三部分：簡短對話聽力詳述解答

（C） 21. **Man:** Have you heard from Kathy?

Woman: No, I haven't seen her for quite a long time.

Man: Neither have I.

Question: What is true according to the conversation?

A. The woman did not know Kathy.

B. The man has seen Kathy recently.

C. Neither of them has seen Kathy recently.

【文法】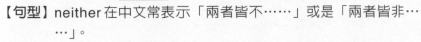

neither + 助動詞 / be動詞 + 某乙 } 表示某乙也不⋯⋯

【句型】 neither 在中文常表示「兩者皆不⋯⋯」或是「兩者皆非⋯⋯」。

（B） 22. **Man:** Are you ready? Let me count to three. Say "Cheese!"

Woman: "Cheese!"

Question: What is the man doing?

A. He is going to buy three pieces of cheese.

B. He is taking a picture of the woman.

C. He makes the woman eat cheese.

（C） 23. **Man:** Hi, Rachel! Guess what?

Woman: What?

Man: I passed the history exam! I can graduate this semester.

Woman: No wonder you look so excited.

Question: Why is the man so excited?

A. He is going to get married.

B. He is going to pass the exam.

C. He is going to graduate.

【單字】graduate (n.) 畢業、畢業生

　　　　semester (n.) 學期

（A）24. **Man:** 2 round-trip tickets to Taichung, please.

　　　　Woman: 450 dollars per ticket. The total is 900 dollars.

　　　　Man: Here is 1,000 dollars.

　　　　Woman: Here are 2 round-trip tickets. Your change, 100 dollars.

　　　　Question: Where does the conversation take place?

　　　　A. A train station.

　　　　B. A gas station.

　　　　C. A post office.

【單字】one-way ticket 單程車票

　　　　round-trip ticket（美式用法）= return ticket（英式用法）來回票

（B） 25. **Man:** Your mom isn't feeling very well, is she?

Woman: No, she is feeling sick. She's just caught a cold.

Man: Did she see a doctor?

Woman: No, she just had some hot lemon juice and honey.

Question: Who has a cold?

A. The man's mom.

B. The woman's mom.

C. The woman who is talking.

（B） 26. **Man:** Let me pick up the bill, Jenny.

Woman: No, you did last time. Let me take care of the bill.

Man: How about going Dutch?

Question: What does the man mean?

A. He is going abroad.

B. He wants to share the bill.

C. He doesn't want to pay for the bill.

【英文常識】 pick up 最基本的意思是撿起來，但還有更多進階的用法。例如可表示順道去買東西，所以 pick up 也可以等於 buy。當 pick up 後面接的是人時，還可以當接載某人的意思。pick up 還有一個比較俚語的用法，雖然在考試較少見，可是在生活上倒是常常聽到這樣的用法。

例如生活中說的 pick up girls = 泡妞，而「吊凱子」的用法亦同。

（B） 27. **Man:** May I take your order, please.

Woman: Yes, a fruit salad and a California sandwich.

Man: Your order will be ready soon.

Question: What does the man do?

A. He is a doctor.

B. He is a waiter.

C. He is a police man.

（B） 28. **Woman:** It is 7 o'clock. You should get up, or you will be late.

Man: Today is Sunday. There is no school.

Woman: Get up and get dressed. We need to go to church.

Question: What is the woman doing?

A. She is sleeping.

B. She is waking up the man.

C. She is going to school.

【解析】or 是連接詞，在此處則表示「否則、不然」。例句可 譯成「已經七點了，你該起床了，不然你會遲到的。」

【解析】no school 不能直接譯成「沒有學校」，而是譯作「不用去上 課」。

（C） 29. **Woman:** Hello! May I talk to Maria?

Man: Maria is out. Would you like to leave a message?

Woman: Yes, please just tell her to call me back. This is Nancy. My phone number is 22327899.

Man: I will tell Maria to call you back at 22327899. Is that right, Nancy?

Woman: Yes, thank you very much.

Question: Whose phone number is 22327899?

A. The man's.

B. Maria's.

C. Nancy's.

名師解析

【英文常識】leave a message 的 leave 表示要留言的意思。
在接聽電話時，留言的動詞用 leave；可是當要求為對方記下留言，記留言的動詞則是用 take。所以，一般我們會跟對方說 Would you like to leave a message?（需要我為你轉達嗎？），或是 Can I take a message? 請注意留言這個動詞，一個是 leave，一個是 take。

(B) 30. **Woman:** I need to take your temperature first.

Man: All right.

Woman: Please wait a minute. Doctor Chang will see you in a moment. There are only two more patients before you. I will call you.

Question: What kind of job does the woman do?

A. She is a patient.

B. She is a nurse.

16

C. She is a teacher.

 名師解析

【片語】量體溫的動詞為 take，take one's temperature 表示
　　　量某人的體溫。

【片語】 wait a minute
　　　 wait a moment ⎬ 表示等一下
　　　 wait a second

【單字】 patient 的形容詞是譯成「耐心的」，而在名詞則是譯成「病
　　　人」。請注意單字在不同詞性時，會有不同的意思及用法，
　　　平常在學新單字時務必小心理解單字的意思。

重點筆記

本測驗分三部份，全部都是單選題，共30題，作答時間約20分鐘。作答說明為中文，印在試題冊上並經由錄音播出。

第一部分：看圖辨義

共10題，每題請聽錄音播出題目和三個英文句子之後，選出與所看到的圖畫最相符的答案。每題只播出一遍。

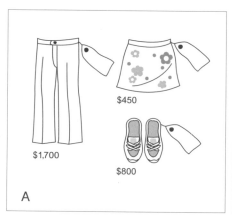

A

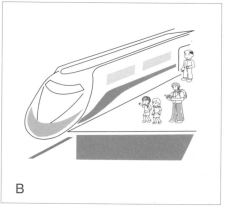

B

C

D

E

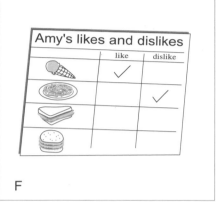

F

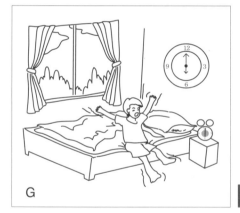

G

考題請翻下一頁 ▶

第二部分：問答

共10題，每題請聽錄音播出的英文句子，再從試題冊上三個回答中，選出一個最適合的答案。每題只播出一遍。

11. A. They will come here.
    B. Oh, I see. I heard about that, too.
    C. Really, I did not go with Mary, either.

12. A. Good luck.
    B. Congratulations!
    C. Never mind.

13. A. No problem.
    B. Sure, thanks.
    C. Can I go with you?

14. A. It was quite easy.
    B. You can say that again.
    C. How come!

15. A. That's cool.
    B. Poor her!
    C. It is pretty good.

16. A. Let's call it a day.
    B. Because I worked very hard.

C. Did your parents get mad about that?

17. A. It is my home.

B. Thanks.

C. When will you go back home?

18. A. What's wrong?

B. Did she pass the exam?

C. Sounds great.

19. A. John asked me.

B. I looked it up in the dictionary.

C. Nobody knows the truth.

20. A. At 7 o'clock sharp.

B. In 1997.

C. Every morning after you brush your teeth.

第三部分：簡短對話

　　共10題，每題請聽錄音播出一段對話和一個相關的問題後，再從試題冊上三個選項中，選出一個最適合的答案。每段對話和問題播出兩遍。

21. A. Look for the train station.

B. Order a large steak.

C. Find a tea house.

22. A. She was drinking coffee all night.
    B. She did nothing.
    C. She made coffee last night.

23. A. A doctor.
    B. A librarian.
    C. A friend.

24. A. Teacher and student in class.
    B. Husband and wife in their bedroom.
    C. Cashier and customer in the supermarket.

25. A. The woman's best friend.
    B. The woman's boss.
    C. He is just a passer-by.

26. A. It is your own business.
    B. Ok. You may call again in an hour.
    C. Who is calling?

27. A. In a police station.
    B. In a clinic.
    C. In a post office.

28. A. On Chinese New Year.
    B. After New Year.

C. On Christmas Eve.

29. A. They are newspaper reporters.
    B. They are professors.
    C. They are students.

30. A. Her mom.
    B. The girl herself.
    C. One hairdresser.

第一部分：看圖辨義聽力詳述解答

(B) 1. For question 1, please look at picture A.

How much are the pants?

A. Seven thousand dollars.

B. Seventeen hundred dollars.

C. Five hundred and fifty dollars.

【單字】pants 褲子（美式用法）＝ trousers 褲子（英式用法）

(A) 2. For question 2, please look at picture A again.

Which item is the most expensive of the three?

A. The pants.

B. The skirt.

C. The shoes.

【單字】item (n.) 品名、項目、商品

(A) 3. For question 3, please look at picture A once again.

According to the picture, how much do both the pants
and the shoes cost?

A. Two thousand five hundred dollars.

B. One thousand seven hundred dollars.

C. Less than one thousand dollars.

【片語】according to 根據……
【單字】less 表示較少、較不……之意
　　　　less than one thousand dollars 可譯成「不到1000元」。

（C）4. For question 4, please look at picture B.

Where are they?

A. They are at the bus station.

B. They are the at the park.

C. They are at the train station.

（C）5. For question 5, please look at picture C.

What are they doing?

A. They are dancing.

B. They are cooking food.

C. They are eating.

（B）6. For question 6, please look at picture D.

Why are they getting in line?

A. They are waiting for a school bus.

B. They are waiting to buy tickets to the theater.

C. They are fighting with each other.

【單字】line (n.) 直線，在此可表示為排隊的意思。

26

（A）7. For question 7, please look at picture E.

What is this?

A. This is a calendar.

B. This is a photo.

C. This is a dictionary.

【單字】calendar (n.) 日曆或月曆

（B）8. For question 8, please look at picture E again.

What day is June 5ᵗʰ?

A. It's Sunday.

B. It's Monday.

C. It's Wednesday.

【英文常識】在表示日期時，是用序數第一、第二、第三、第四、第五，就是 first / second / third / fourth / fifth，所以六月五號就要說成六月的第五天，即 June 5ᵗʰ.

（A）9. For question 9, please look at picture F.

What does Amy dislike?

A. Only noodles.

B. Ice cream and hamburgers.

C. Noodles and Sandwiches.

【單字】dislike 注意不要跟 unlike 混淆，dislike 為動詞，表
「不喜歡」；unlike 則是「不像」。

【單字】noodles (n.) 麵條，單字使用上多為複數型，因為麵通常不
會只有一條，所以大多都是加 s。

（A） 10. For question 10, please look at picture G.

What time does the boy get up?

A. At six o'clock.

B. At nine o'clock.

C. At noon.

【片語】get up（起床），和 wake up（醒來）是相似的用法。

第二部分：問答聽力詳述解答

（B） 11. The newspaper said Taipei 101 opened last Sunday.

A. They will come here.

B. Oh, I see. I heard about that, too.

C. Really, I did not go with Mary, either.

【單字】一般講「報章雜誌上說：……」的「說」即是 say 這
個字，和中文的用法大同小異。

（C）12.I am sorry I am late.

　　　　A. Good luck.

　　　　B. Congratulations!

　　　　C. Never mind.

【單字】congratulations 表示恭喜，這個字以複數型表示，因
　　　　為通常中文恭喜是不只一次的，所以要加 s。

（C）13.We are going to see a movie.

　　　　A. No problem.

　　　　B. Sure, thanks.

　　　　C. Can I go with you?

（A）14.How was the final exam yesterday?

　　　　A. It was quite easy.

　　　　B. You can say that again.

　　　　C. How come!

【句型】You can say that again. 逐字翻譯是「你可以再說一
　　　　次」，但事實上是「我也這麼認為」或「當然我也這麼認為」
　　　　之意。表示認同那個人所說的話，例如：有人說台灣是一個
　　　　很美的島── Taiwan is a beautiful island. 身為台灣人，你可
　　　　以說 You can say that again. 就是「的確我也這麼覺得。」

（B）15. Jenny has no friends.

      A. That's cool.

      B. Poor her.

      C. It is pretty good.

（C）16. I got a very bad grade on my English test.

      A. Let's call it a day.

      B. Because I worked very hard.

      C. Did your parents get mad about that?

【單字】grade 這個字可以當年級、成績，因為以前成績不好
      的話，就沒辦法升級。

（B）17. Please make yourself at home.

      A. It is my home.

      B. Thanks.

      C. When will you go back home?

【解析】Make yourself at home.「當作你在自己家裡」是一
      個慣用的片語，意思表示放輕鬆、不要拘束之意。

（A）18. Kathy stays in the hospital.

      A. What's wrong?

      B. Did she pass the exam?

      C. Sounds great.

（B） 19. How did you get the meaning of this word?

　　　　A. John asked me.

　　　　B. I looked it up in the dictionary.

　　　　C. Nobody knows the truth.

【片語】look...up 查閱

　　　look up 單字／片語 in the dictionary， 即是用字典查單字片語的意思。

（A） 20. What time does the concert start?

　　　　A. At 7 o'clock sharp.

　　　　B. In 1997.

　　　　C. Every morning after you brush your teeth.

【單字】sharp 有「尖銳」之意，sharp 擺在幾點鐘的後面即有「整點」之意，所以 at 7 o'clock sharp，就是「七點整」的意思。

第三部分：簡短對話聽力詳述解答

（C） 21. **Man:** It is so hot today. I am very thirsty.

　　　　Woman: Me, too. Let's get something to drink.

　　　　Question: What are they most likely going to do next?

　　　　A. Look for the train station.

B. Order a large steak.

C. Find a tea house.

【單字】like (v.) (prep) 可當動詞表示「喜歡」，也可當介係詞
表示「像……」。

alike (adj.) 相像的

likely (adj.) (adv.) 可能的或可能地

order 可以表示「次序」，也可以當「點菜」。點菜、訂貨、
訂單、次序，都可以用 order 表示。

（B）22. **Woman:** I did not sleep well last night.

Man: What did you do?

Woman: Nothing. I drank too much coffee yesterday
afternoon.

Question: What did the woman do last night?

A. She was drinking coffee all night.

B. She did nothing.

C. She made coffee last night.

（B）23. **Woman:** This morning there was a call for you from the
public library.

Man: About what?

Woman: The books you borrowed were due last week.

Question: Who called the man this morning?

A. A doctor.

B. A librarian.

C. A friend.

【片語】borrow...from... 從……借來……

lend...to... 借……給……

due to... = because of... 因為……、由於……

due 到期

(B) 24. **Woman:** Do you hear the noise, honey?

Man: Yeah. (Sounds sleepy.)

Woman: Can you get up to ask them to turn down the music? It is midnight!

Man: Honey, I am so tired. Can you get up to tell them?

Question: Who are they and where are they?

A. Teacher and student in class.

B. Husband and wife in their bedroom.

C. Cashier and customer in the supermarket.

【片語】turn down 表示把聲音關小聲，turn up 則表示開大聲。turn on 打開電器，turn off 是指關掉任何的電器產品。

【單字】cashier (n.) 出納員

customer (n.) 顧客

【解析】從語氣中可以判斷他們的關係很親密，尤其在對話中有 midnight（深夜），可以作為讓聽者知道他們之間關係的 clue（線索）。通常是很親密的人才會稱作 honey、sweetheart；darling 則表示出二人之間有更親密的關係。

（C） 25. **Woman:** Excuse me, could you tell me how to get to the nearest MRT station?

Man: I am a stranger here. Sorry!

Woman: Thank you, anyway.

Question: Who is the man?

A. The woman's best friend.

B. The woman's boss.

C. He is just a passer-by.

 名 師 解 析

【單字】MRT= Mass Rapid Transit，逐字翻譯是大眾快速來往的交通工具，簡稱做 MRT，即捷運。

（B） 26. **Woman:** May I speak to Mr. Hwang, please?

Man: He is not in. Would you like to leave a message?

Woman: No, thanks. I will call him later.

Question: What will the man say next?

A. It is your own business.

B. Ok. You may call again in an hour.

C. Who is calling?

 名 師 解 析

【解析】A 選項的 business 可以當事業、生意，但當我們說 It's your own business 則表示「那是你自己的事情，與我無關」，所以答案不可能是 A。而 B 選項的 in+ 時間，表示「在一段時間後立即⋯⋯」。如：I will be back in three hours. 表示「我會在三小時後即回來」的意思。C 選項是問「是誰打電話來？」

（B） 27. **Man:** Good morning, Mrs. Lin. How are you feeling now?

Woman: Not very well, I have a sore throat and a runny nose.

Man: Let me check if you have a fever.

Question: Where does the conversation take place?

A. In a police station.

B. In a clinic.

C. In a post office.

名師解析

【單字】check (v.) 可以表示檢查、看一看，(n.) 又可以當支票。

延伸單字： sore throat 喉嚨痛　　　back aches 背部痛

fever 發高燒、發燒　　runny nose 流鼻涕

cough 咳嗽　　　　　clinic 診所

（C） 28. **Man:** Merry Christmas, Joanna!

Woman: Merry Christmas, Timothy! Where do you plan to go on vacation?

Man: My wife and I will go to Hawaii and stay a whole week. How about you?

Woman: I will visit my parents in New York.

Question: When is the conversation probably happening?

A. On Chinese New Year.

B. After New Year.

C. On Christmas Eve.

（C）29. **Man:** Let's go to a movie tonight!

Woman: No, I can't go with you. I have to write a lot of papers.

Man: I just finished mine. I can help you with those papers after we come back. So come on!

Woman: I am afraid Professor Chang will know they were not written by me.

Question: What do they do?

A. They are newspaper reporters.

B. They are professors.

C. They are students.

名師解析

【單字】paper 有非常多的意思，當紙張為不可數名詞；當報
　　　紙、論文、報告文件則是以加 s 的複數型 papers 表示。
　　　reporter (n.) 報導者或記者
　　　professor (n.) 教授

（C）30. **Man:** I couldn't help but stare at your new hair style. It looks so great. It suits you.

Woman: Really? I just had my hair done last night.

Man: So did it cost you a lot?

Woman: My mom paid for it.

Question: Who did the woman's hair last night?

A. Her mom.

B. The girl herself.

C. A hairdresser.

【單字】hair style (n.) 髮型。

【片語】有禁不住、忍不住意思的片語有：

　　① can't but

　　② can't choose but

　　③ can't help

　　④ can't help but

重點筆記

本測驗分三部份，全部都是單選題，共30題，作答時間約20分鐘。作答說明為中文，印在試題冊上並經由錄音播出。

第一部分：看圖辨義

共10題，每題請聽錄音播出題目和三個英文句子之後，選出與所看到的圖畫最相符的答案。每題只播出一遍。

A

B

C

D

E

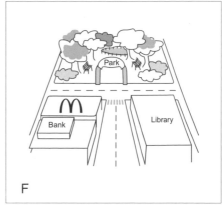

F

G

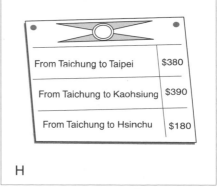

H

考題請翻下一頁 ▶

第二部分：問答

共10題，每題請聽錄音播出的英文句子，再從試題冊上三個回答中，選出一個最適合的答案。每題只播出一遍。

11. A. Yes, I am looking for a tie to go with the shirt.
    B. Thank you very much.
    C. I will help you with the work.

12. A. Every day.
    B. For many years.
    C. I don't like English at all.

13. A. I will be glad to.
    B. No one will go.
    C. Whose birthday?

14. A. I will go on a picnic tomorrow.
    B. I will go there by MRT.
    C. Terrific!

15. A. Yes, but it took a lot of time.
    B. I feel puzzled.
    C. It is a puzzle.

16. A. Yes, I would like to.
    B. No, I am very hungry now.

C. Thank you, anyway.

17. A. Yes, she has been there many times.

B. No, she was in Hong Kong last year.

C. Yes, she has been living in Taiwan.

18. A. I am a teacher.

B. Great, thanks!

C. I do nothing.

19. A. I live in an apartment.

B. One living room, and two bedrooms with two bathrooms.

C. Why did you buy the house?

20. A. Sure. It is ten.

B. Where are you going?

C. What are you doing?

第三部分：簡短對話

共10題，每題請聽錄音播出一段對話和一個相關的問題後，再從試題冊上三個選項中，選出一個最適合的答案。每段對話和問題播出<u>兩遍</u>。

21. A. He is very hungry.

B. He is riding a horse.

C. He is going to eat a horse.

22. A. One kind of food.

   B. The names of some countries.

   C. A kind of music.

23. A. Their boss.

   B. Their father.

   C. Their neighbor.

24. A. On the train.

   B. In the department store.

   C. In class.

25. A. How nice a day!

   B. I go to the movies about once every two months.

   C. Sorry, I can't go to a movie with you.

26. A. She couldn't hear clearly.

   B. She wants to say thanks to the man.

   C. She hates the man who made a noise.

27. A. The man hopes Jenny has a car accident again.

   B. The man doesn't know who Jenny is.

   C. It was not the first time that Jenny had a car accident.

28. A. At a police station.

   B. At a book store.

C. At a park.

29. A. You are welcome.
    B. It is so rude to say that.
    C. It takes 20 minutes to get to my school.

30. A. On an airplane.
    B. On a train.
    C. On a bicycle.

第一部分：看圖辨義聽力詳述解答

(C) 1. For question 1, please look at picture A.

What is true?

A. One of the girls is playing the guitar.

B. Both the girls are playing the guitar.

C. The boy is playing the guitar and the girls are singing.

(A) 2. For question 2, please look at picture B.

What is the girl trying on?

A. A hat.

B. Shoes.

C. Socks.

【片語】try on 試穿、聯想的

【單字】fitting room (n.) 試穿室

(A) 3. For question 3, please look at picture C.

What does he do?

A. He is a postman.

B. He is a policeman.

C. He is a gentleman.

(C) 4. For question 4, please look at picture C again.

What is the man doing?

A. He is writing a letter.

B. He is delivering pizza.

C. He is delivering mail.

【單字】deliver newspapers / pizza / mail，即送報紙、送披薩或送郵件。

（B） 5. For question 5, please look at picture D.

What is the girl doing?

A. She is watering the plants in the garden.

B. She is cooking in the kitchen.

C. She is washing dishes in the kitchen.

【單字】water 可作為動詞，to water the plants 是澆花的意思。

（B） 6. For question 6, please look at picture E.

What is the man in the middle doing?

A. He is reading a book.

B. He is reading a newspaper.

C. He is sleeping.

（C） 7. For question 7, please look at picture F.

Where is the bank?

A. It is across from the park.

B. It is beside the library.

C. It is beside the McDonald's.

(C) 8. For question 8, please look at picture F again.

Where is the library?

A. It is behind the park.

B. It is between the park and the McDonald's.

C. It is across from the McDonald's.

【片語】across from 表示「在……的對面」。

(B) 9. For question 9, please look at picture G.

What is the boy doing?

A. He is eating lunch.

B. He is eating breakfast.

C. He is eating dinner.

(B) 10. For question 10, please look at picture H.

Which trip costs the most?

A. From Taichung to Taipei.

B. From Taichung to Kaohsiung.

C. From Taichung to Hsinchu.

【單字】trip (n.) 旅行或一趟路程。

第二部分：問答聽力詳述解答

（A） 11. May I help you?

A. Yes, I am looking for a tie to go with the shirt.

B. Thank you very much.

C. I will help you with the work.

 名 師 解 析

【片語】go with 逐字翻譯是「跟……走在一起」，可延伸為「搭配」或「適配」。

（B） 12. How long have you studied English?

A. Every day.

B. For many years.

C. I don't like English at all.

（A） 13. Tomorrow is my birthday. Will you come to the party?

A. I will be glad to.

B. No one will go.

C. Whose birthday?

（C） 14. How did you feel about the movie?

A. I will go on a picnic tomorrow.

B. I will go there by MRT.

C. Terrific!

【單字】C選項中的 terrific 表示「很棒很棒」的意思，因為乍看之下非常相像，請不要與 terrible 混淆了。

（A） 15. Wow! You have finished the puzzle.

      A. Yes, but it took a lot of time.

      B. I feel puzzled.

      C. It is a puzzle.

【解析】在B選項中 puzzle 加了 ed，表示「困惑的」，而C選項的 a puzzle 是指拼圖遊戲。

（B） 16. Did you have lunch yet?

      A. Yes, I would like to.

      B. No, I am very hungry now.

      C. Thank you, anyway.

【解析】答案為B，直接回答對方說「還沒，我現在覺得很餓」。而C選項是常聽的句子，當對方說 Thank you, anyway. 時表示另一方並沒有達成對方的請求，所以他說「總而言之謝謝你」，這同時也是在考試中可參考的線索。

（A） 17. Has Mrs. Huang ever been to Hong Kong?

      A. Yes, she has been there many times.

B. No, she was in Hong Kong last year.

C. Yes, she has been living in Taiwan.

（B） 18. How are you doing?

　　　A. I am a teacher.

　　　B. Great, thanks!

　　　C. I do nothing.

（B） 19. How many rooms are there in your apartment?

　　　A. I live in an apartment.

　　　B. One living room, and two bedrooms with two bathrooms.

　　　C. Why did you buy the house?

【單字】apartment (n.) 公寓，請不要跟 department 混淆，
　　　department (n.) 為科系、部門之意。

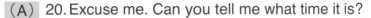

（A） 20. Excuse me. Can you tell me what time it is?

　　　A. Sure. It is ten.

　　　B. Where are you going?

　　　C. What are you doing?

【解析】A 選項主詞是 It is...，be 動詞後面接數字是指幾點
　　　鐘，問的是時間，所以答案為 A。如果是人 +be 動詞 + 數字
　　　時，主詞是人時，則數字是指歲數。

第三部分：簡短對話聽力詳述解答

(A) 21. **Woman:** Are you hungry?

Man: I am hungry enough to eat a horse.

Question: What does the man mean?

A. He is very hungry.

B. He is riding a horse.

C. He is going to eat a horse.

名 師 解 析

【英語常識】中文表示非常飢餓時常說「餓的可以吃下一頭
牛」，英文也有相似的表達，hungry enough to eat a
horse（餓的足以吃下一匹馬），和中文是大同小異的，
只是要注意比喻用的動物是不一樣的。

(A) 22. **Woman:** Have you ever eaten a bagel?

Man: No, what is it?

Woman: It is from America. It is like a kind of bread.

Question: What are they talking about?

A. One kind of food.

B. The names of some countries.

C. A kind of music.

名 師 解 析

【單字】bagel (n.) 貝果，是種硬麵包。

（C）23. **Woman:** Miss Hwang just moved out of our apartment building last month.

Man: Did she? I did not know. What a pity! She is so nice and always so helpful in our community. I will miss her.

Question: Who are they talking about?

A. Their boss.

B. Their father.

C. Their neighbor.

【單字】What a pity! 好可惜啊！多麼可惜啊！

community (n.) 社區

（B）24. **Man:** Can I help you, Madam?

Woman: No. Thanks! I am just browsing.

Question: Where are they?

A. On the train.

B. In the department store.

C. In class.

【單字】madam (n.) 是對女士的一種尊稱。

browse (v.) 不經意的瀏覽、沒有目的的看一看。

（B）25. **Woman:** It has been quite a long time since I last saw a movie. I like going to movies, but I have been too busy to see a movie.

Man: How often do you go to the movies?

Question: What will the woman probably answer?

A. How nice a day!

B. I go to the movies about once every two months.

C. Sorry, I can't go to a movie with you.

【句型】too + 形容詞或副詞 + to + 原形動詞，表示太……而不……

How often 問頻率。

（A）26. **Woman:** What's your name, please?

Man: My name is Jonathan Clinton.

Woman: Pardon? It is too noisy here.

Question: What does the woman mean?

A. She couldn't hear clearly.

B. She wants to say thanks to the man.

C. She hates the man who made a noise.

【解析】pardon 字面上是「對不起，請求原諒」，但在日常生活中，當這個字出現音調提高時，表示「對不起，請再說一次好嗎？」。而製造噪音的動詞用 make，make a noise 就是「製造噪音」。

（C）27. **Woman:** Have you heard from Jenny?

Man: No, I haven't. How is she?

Woman: She was hurt in a car accident last week.

Man: What! Again?

Question: What is true?

A. The man hopes Jenny has a car accident again.

B. The man doesn't know who Jenny is.

C. It was not the first time that Jenny had a car accident.

【片語】 hear from +某人，表示「有某人的消息」。

（B）28. **Man:** Excuse me, Miss. Where can I find the bestsellers for English learning?

Woman: They are on the second floor. As soon as you get out of the elevator, you will find them on the first shelf to the right.

Question: Where are they?

A. At a police station.

B. At a book store.

C. At a park.

【單字】 bestseller 切開這個字 best / seller，字面上是最好的／銷售者，其實表示「暢銷書」的意思。

（C）29. **Man:** How do you go to school?

Woman: By bus.

Man: How long does it take to get to your school by bus?

Question: What will the woman most likely answer?

A. You are welcome.

B. It is so rude to say that.

C. It takes 20 minutes to get to my school.

【片語】most likely 最有可能的。

（B）30. **Man:** Excuse me. May I see your ticket, please?

Woman: Sure. Here you are. By the way, how many stations will we pass before we get to Tainan?

Man: Only 2 stations. You need to get off after 2 stations.

Question: Where are they?

A. On an airplane.

B. On a train.

C. On a bicycle.

【片語】get off 下車或指離開大型的交通工具，若是指一般的車子或小型車用 get out。

本測驗分三部份，全部都是單選題，共 30 題，作答時間約 20 分鐘。作答說明為中文，印在試題冊上並經由錄音播出。

第一部分：看圖辨義

共 10 題，每題請聽錄音播出題目和三個英文句子之後，選出與所看到的圖畫最相符的答案。每題只播出一遍。

A

B

C

D

E

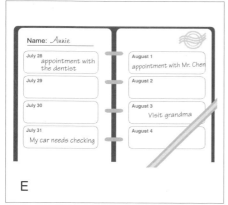

F

G

H

考題請翻下一頁 ▶

第二部分：問答

共10題，每題請聽錄音播出的英文句子，再從試題冊上三個回答中，選出一個最適合的答案。每題只播出一遍。

11. A. Yes, she likes coffee.
    B. Yes, please.
    C. No, just one cup.

12. A. The line is very busy.
    B. Who will answer the question?
    C. I am sorry. I went to see a movie with my mom.

13. A. Nice to meet you, too.
    B. OK. I will.
    C. Hello, Mom and Dad!

14. A. What is the National Palace Museum?
    B. Sorry, you can not talk to me.
    C. Go straight. It's just down the road.

15. A. I will study hard.
    B. I can hardly get up.
    C. Take an umbrella.

16. A. Thank you so much.
    B. You are so popular.

C. I had a toothache.

17. A. Oops! Sorry, I forgot to return them.

    B. I didn't like studying in the library.

    C. When is the baby due?

18. A. I had a math question.

    B. I had a fever and a bad cough.

    C. Can you do me a favor?

19. A. I have heard a lot about you.

    B. I cannot hear you.

    C. Is he a famous movie star?

20. A. She should eat more.

    B. She needs to go on a diet.

    C. She puts on a new pair of glasses.

第三部分：簡短對話

共 10 題，每題請聽錄音播出一段對話和一個相關的問題後，再從試題冊上三個選項中，選出一個最適合的答案。每段對話和問題播出<u>兩遍</u>。

21. A. Father and mother.

    B. Two good friends.

    C. Brother and sister.

22. A. Puppy love.

    B. Keeping a pet.

    C. Their family.

23. A. Nobody will help the man.

    B. She has no idea how to get to Central Shopping Mall.

    C. She has no family.

24. A. She is dying.

    B. She is going to pass out.

    C. She has no ink.

25. A. Ask Laura to stop working part time.

    B. Ask Laura to work.

    C. Ask Laura for dinner.

26. A. The man will go to the party.

    B. The man cannot go to the party.

    C. The man has an appointment with the woman tonight.

27. A. In a bakery.

    B. In a post office.

    C. In a car.

28. A. His car is broken.

    B. He is sick.

C. His mom is ill.

29. A. A nurse in a hospital.
    B. A teller in a bank.
    C. A florist.

30. A. The woman has been in Taiwan for 6 years.
    B. The woman thinks Chinese is very easy.
    C. The woman can speak very good Taiwanese.

第一部分：看圖辨義聽力詳述解答

(B) 1. For question 1, please look at picture A.
        What are the lady and her dog doing?
        A. They are walking along the street.
        B. They are walking across the street.
        C. They are crossing the river.

名師解析

【解析】圖中，女人與狗並不是沿著（walk along）街道而
        行，而是穿越馬路（walk across）。
【單字】river (n.) 河流

(A) 2. For question 2, please look at picture B.
        Where are they?
        A. They are at the train station.
        B. They are in a car.
        C. They are in front of a bank.

(A) 3. For question 3, please look at picture B again.
        What time is it?
        A. It is eight forty.
        B. It is four eighty.
        C. It is eight fourteen.

(B) 4. For question 4, please look at picture C.

Where is the woman?

A. She is in a library.

B. She is at a market.

C. She is in a movie theater.

(B) 5. For question 5, please look at picture D.

What does the sign mean?

A. Do not swim.

B. Do not smoke.

C. Do not park any cars here.

(A) 6. For question 6, please look at picture E.

What date will Annie have an appointment with a dentist?

A. July 28th.

B. July 31st.

C. August 1st.

 名 師 解 析

【單字】appointment (n.) 約會、約定，前面常搭配動詞 make，appointment 指非男女間的約會，大多是正式的約會或與醫生預約時間，而男女情侶的約會為 date (n.)。

dentist (n.) 牙醫師

(C) 7. For question 7, please look at picture E again.

What date will Annie pay a visit to her grandma?

A. August 13th.

B. August 30ᵗʰ.

C. August 3ʳᵈ.

【片語】visit... = pay a visit to... 拜訪……

（B） 8. For question 8, please look at picture F.

What does the man do?

A. He is a bank cashier.

B. He is a policeman.

C. He is a postman.

【單字】cashier = teller（出納員），cash（現金）＋ ier 之後，
即為收、發現金的工作者，通常指在銀行、公司或商店的出
納員，而 teller（出納員）的用法，僅用於銀行裡。

（C） 9. For question 9, please look at picture G.

How does the boy go to school?

A. By car.

B. By bus.

C. By bicycle.

（A） 10. For question 10, please look at picture H.

Who is the shortest?

A. Linda is.

B. Alan is.

C. Tom is.

第二部分：問答聽力詳述解答

（B） 11. Would you like a cup of coffee?

      A. Yes, she likes coffee.

      B. Yes, please.

      C. No, just one cup.

【句型】Would you like...? = Do you want...?

（C） 12. I called you last night, but no one answered the phone.

      A. The line is very busy.

      B. Who will answer the question?

      C. I am sorry. I went to see a movie with my mom.

（B） 13. Please say hello to your parents.

      A. Nice to meet you, too.

      B. OK. I will.

      C. Hello, Mom and Dad!

【解析】Please say hello to your parents.較正式用法可以是 Please send my regards to your parents.（請代我問候你的 父母）。

(C) 14. Can you show me how to get to the National Palace Museum?

A. What is the National Palace Museum?

B. Sorry, you can not talk to me.

C. Go straight. It's just down the road.

【單字】national (adj.) 國立的、全國的
palace (n.) 宮殿、皇宮
museum (n.) 博物館
National Palace Museum (n.) 指故宮博物院，是一個重要的
地標，同時也是各考試的最愛哦！

(C) 15. It's raining hard.

A. I will study hard.

B. I can hardly get up.

C. Take an umbrella.

(A) 16. The gift is for you.

A. Thank you so much.

B. You are so popular.

C. I had a toothache.

(A) 17. I am calling to remind you the books you borrowed are overdue.

A. Oops! Sorry, I forgot to return them.

B. I didn't like studying in the library.

C. When is the baby due?

【單字】overdue (adj.) 過期的

【句型】remind 人 (that 可省略) S+V 　提醒某人……

【解析】C 選項表示「這嬰兒的預產期在什麼時候」

(B) 18. Why did you go to see the doctor?

A. I had a math question.

B. I had a fever and a bad cough.

C. Can you do me a favor?

(C) 19. Have you heard about Tom Cruise?

A. I have heard a lot about you.

B. I cannot hear you.

C. Is he a famous movie star?

【片語】hear of... = hear about... 聽說過……

　　　A hear from B　A 有 B 的消息

(B) 20. Mary has put on 10 kilograms lately.

A. She should eat more.

B. She needs to go on a diet.

C. She puts on a new pair of glasses.

【片語】put on + 重量 = gain 增加重量
　　　　take off + 重量 = lose 減少重量

第三部分：簡短對話聽力詳述解答

(C) 21. **Woman:** Woo..., I've got you. You are smoking. I am going to tell Mom.

　　　 Man: You wouldn't dare. O.K. Here is 100 dollars. You can buy anything you want. Just don't tell Mom.

　　　 Question: Who are they?

　　　 A. Father and mother.

　　　 B. Two good friends.

　　　 C. Brother and sister.

【單字】dare（膽敢），在疑問句、否定句中常作助動詞，後接動詞原形，但在此為一般動詞的用法。

(B) 22. **Man:** Mom, can I have a dog?

　　　 Woman: No way, you don't even know how to take care of yourself.

　　　 Man: Don't worry. I will take good care of myself and the puppy. Besides, everyone in the family can help me to look after it.

　　　 Question: What are they talking about?

A. Puppy love.

B. Keeping a pet.

C. Their family.

【片語】take care of = look after 照顧

【單字】puppy (n.) 小狗

【單字】besides... 除了……，還有……

beside... 在……旁邊

（besides 請勿與 beside 混為一談）

(B) 23. **Man:** Excuse me, how can I find Central Shopping Mall?

Woman: Sorry, I can't help you. I am not familiar with the area.

Question: What does the woman mean?

A. Nobody will help the man.

B. She has no idea how to get to Central Shopping Mall.

C. She has no family.

【句型】人 + be familiar with + 事物 ⎫
事物 + be familiar to + 人 ⎭ 人對某些事物感到熟悉

familiar 由 family（家庭）變化而來，對自家（家庭）的東西，當然熟悉囉！

【單字】mall (n.) 在美國，此字表示一排商店或在幾個社區附近會有幾家商店或餐館聚集處，但在其他地區用法較廣泛，可指大型購物中心。

70

(C) 24. **Man:** Do you have any ink for the printer?

Woman: We have run out of ink.

Question: What does the woman mean?

A. She is dying.

B. She is going to pass out.

C. She has no ink now.

【片語】run out of... 1.用光……

2.缺貨……

(A) 25. **Woman:** Laura got a part-time job.

Man: Don't you think she needs to study harder? I don't think it is a good idea. I need to talk to her.

Woman: Yes, you are right. She needs to spend more time studying. She will be back home in an hour. Tell her to quit.

Question: What does the woman want the man to do?

A. Ask Laura to stop working part time.

B. Ask Laura to work.

C. Ask Laura for dinner.

【單字】quit 與 stop 意思相同，quit 也可以指離職不幹了。

【句型】stop

prevent ＋ 某人 ＋ from 阻止某人不要……

keep

（B）26. **Woman:** Tonight we are going to have a party. Will you join us?

Man: I wish I could. But I have another appointment.

Question: What is true?

A. The man will go to the party.

B. The man cannot go to the party.

C. The man has an appointment with the woman tonight.

【句型】人 wish (that) S + V，此人所希望……(但與事實相反) 所以 I wish I could，表示「我希望我能夠……」，但事實上不能夠的。所以邀約時，要是聽到對方說 I wish I could 的話，就可立即知道對方不能夠去參加了。

（C）27. **Woman:** Fasten your seatbelt. The police are in front of us.

Man: Oops! Thanks for reminding me, darling.

Question: Where is the conversation taking place?

A. In a bakery.

B. In a post office.

C. In a car.

【單字】 fasten (v.) 繫上
　　　seatbelt (n.) 安全帶

【解析】 不是在車上，就是飛機上，才會有 seatbelt，所以下次聽到 seatbelt，可從選項中找 airplane 或 car。

72

（B）28. **Woman:** Can I talk to Mr. Wilson, please?

Man: This is Mr. Wilson speaking.

Woman: Daniel isn't feeling well and he has a fever. He can't go to school today.

Man: That's too bad. I hope he will get better soon.

Question: What's wrong with Daniel?

A. His car is broken.

B. He is sick.

C. His mom is ill.

【解析】well 多為副詞用法，在表達健康無恙時可當形容詞。

【單字】fever (n.) 發燒

broken (adj.) 指壞掉了，機械壞掉了。千萬不可用 bad，bad 為品質不好，在此 bad = poor。

（C）29. **Man:** I am going to visit a female friend in the hospital. Can you help me to pick out some flowers?

Woman: How old is she?

Man: She is a young lady.

Woman: How about these red roses or these sunflowers. Red roses are very popular. Some young ladies also like sunflowers. What do you think?

Question: What is the woman?

A. A nurse in a hospital.

B. A teller in a bank.

C. A florist.

【單字】female (n.) (adj.) 女性、雌性的

popular (adj.) 受歡迎的

florist (n.) 花商、花店主人

(A) 30. **Man:** How long have you stayed in Taiwan?

Woman: I have been here for 6 years.

Man: So you can speak Chinese or Taiwanese now.

Woman: Are you kidding me? Chinese and Taiwanese

are both so difficult.

Question: What is true according to the conversation?

A. The woman has been in Taiwan for 6 years.

B. The woman thinks Chinese is very easy.

C. The woman can speak very good Taiwanese.

【句型】Are you kidding me? 你在跟我開玩笑？

【片語】according to... (prep.) 根據⋯⋯

本測驗分三部份，全部都是單選題，共30題，作答時間約20分鐘。作答說明為中文，印在試題冊上並經由錄音播出。

第一部分：看圖辨義

共10題，每題請聽錄音播出題目和三個英文句子之後，選出與所看到的圖畫最相符的答案。每題只播出一遍。

A

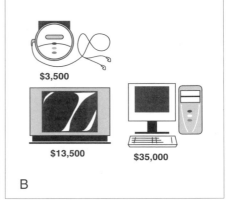

B

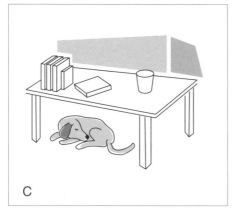

C

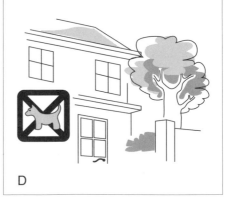

D

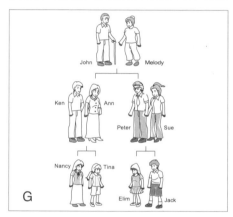

E

F

G

Time Bus to	Depart at	Arrive at
Tainan	2:20	4:35
Chiayi	2:35	4:10
Changhua	2:40	3:20

H

考題請翻下一頁 ▶

第二部分：問答

共 10 題，每題請聽錄音播出的英文句子，再從試題冊上三個回答中，選出一個最適合的答案。每題只播出一遍。

11. A. Me, too. I have heard a lot about you.
    B. Do you think so?
    C. It is nice to have a best friend like you.

12. A. I went to my grandma's and stayed with her.
    B. I have been pretty busy.
    C. I will go fishing with my son.

13. A. I 'd love to, but I have a lot of homework to do.
    B. Will you go hunting?
    C. Do you like dancing?

14. A. Sure, go ahead.
    B. You can not call anyone.
    C. As long as you return it back to me.

15. A. You need to bring a raincoat.
    B. You need a jacket.
    C. Why don't you turn on the air conditioner?

16. A. Yes, let's go.
    B. Well, don't be kidding.

C. Are you sure?

17. A. I spent the vacation with my family.

   B. There are 10 people.

   C. Where is it?

18. A. Do not worry about my test.

   B. Don't worry. I will do it.

   C. Don't you remember my name?

19. A. I like the Melody.

   B. She is not in.

   C. Melody is a sweet girl.

20. A. I will drink more water.

   B. Will you get a cold?

   C. I will bring my umbrella.

第三部分：簡短對話

共 10 題，每題請聽錄音播出一段對話和一個相關的問題後，再從試題冊上三個選項中，選出一個最適合的答案。每段對話和問題播出<u>兩遍</u>。

21. A. They are dancing.

   B. They are on vacation.

   C. They are buying clothes.

22. A. They are stuck in a traffic jam.

    B. They are stuck in the elevator.

    C. They are stuck in the mud.

23. A. A night market.

    B. Clothing.

    C. A brand of a car.

24. A. They are in a kitchen.

    B. They are in a supermarket.

    C. They are in a clinic.

25. A. He feels sick.

    B. He can not hear.

    C. He feels down.

26. A. He loves eating breakfast every day.

    B. He is sick and he doesn't feel hungry.

    C. He doesn't like eating cereal with milk.

27. A. He fixed the clock in the morning.

    B. He didn't sleep until three o'clock in the morning.

    C. He didn't eat anything in the morning.

28. A. They are mad.

    B. They want to buy a map.

C. They are lost.

29. A. They are going jogging.

    B. They are traveling in China.

    C. They are watching a TV program.

30. A. They are about to break up.

    B. They are about to talk to Jenny next.

    C. They are about to go out for lunch.

第一部分：看圖辨義聽力詳述解答

(C) 1. For question 1, please look at picture A.

What does the strongest man wear?

A. He wears a cap.

B. He wears a pair of glasses.

C. He wears a pair of shorts.

【單字】shorts (n.) = short pants (n.) 短褲

(A) 2. For question 2, please look at picture B.

What costs thirteen thousand five hundred dollars?

A. The TV set.

B. The MP3 player.

C. The computer.

(B) 3. For question 3, please look at picture B again.

What costs less than ten thousand dollars?

A. The TV set.

B. The MP3 player.

C. The computer.

【片語】less than... 少於……

（A）4. For question 4, please look at picture C.

Where is the dog?

A. It is under the desk.

B. It is on the desk.

C. It is in the desk.

（B）5. For question 5, please look at picture D.

What does the sign mean?

A. Do not eat a dog.

B. No dogs are allowed to enter.

C. Do not talk about a dog.

【單字】allow (v.) 允許

（B）6. For question 6, please look at picture E.

What is the woman cleaning with?

A. A mop.

B. A vacuum cleaner.

C. A washing machine.

【解析】with + 工具，工具的使用為"with"

【單字】vacuum cleaner (n.) 吸塵器

(B) 7. For question 7, please look at picture F.

What is the little girl doing?

A. She is cutting her own hair.

B. She is having her hair cut.

C. She is cutting the man's hair.

【句型】have her hair cut 是 have + 物 + p.p. 的句型，表示頭髮被剪。而被誰剪呢？此種句型並無明確是被誰剪，但一定不是主詞自己了！

(B) 8. For question 8, please look at picture G.

How many grandsons do John and Melody have?

A. Two grandsons.

B. Only one grandson.

C. Five grandsons.

(B) 9. For question 9, please look at picture G again.

Who is Ann?

A. Peter's mother.

B. Peter's sister.

C. John's wife.

(A) 10. For question 10, please look at picture H.

What time does the bus leave for Tainan?

A. Two twenty.

B. Two thirty-five.

C. Four thirty-five.

第二部分：問答聽力詳述解答

（A）11. Nice to meet you, Mr. Lin.

A. Me, too. I have heard a lot about you.

B. Do you think so?

C. It is nice to have a best friend like you.

【句型】me, too 在此處即可以等於 Nice to meet you, too.，
而 heard a lot about + 某人為「久仰其名」。

（C）12. What's your plan for this coming weekend?

A. I went to my grandma's home and stayed with her.

B. I have been pretty busy.

C. I will go fishing with my son.

【解析】B 選項中 pretty 指的是 (adv.) 相當地，並不是表示美麗
的 (adj.)。

（A）13. We will have a barbecue at Tina's house tonight. Will
you come?

A. I 'd love to, but I have a lot of homework to do.

B. Will you go hunting?

C. Do you like dancing?

（A） 14. May I use your bathroom?

    A. Sure, go ahead.

    B. You can not call anyone.

    C. As long as you return it back to me.

 名 師 解 析

【解析】答案是 A ，表示「請，請便。」。中文在說「借」洗
手間，千萬不要用 borrow ，除非你是要把馬桶抱走。

（C） 15. It is so hot today.

    A. You need to bring a raincoat.

    B. You need a jacket.

    C. Why don't you turn on the air conditioner?

 名 師 解 析

【單字】air conditioner (n.) 空調機、冷氣機

（A） 16. We are going to be late. Can we leave now?

    A. Yes, let's go.

    B. Well, don't be kidding.

    C. Are you sure?

（A）17. Where have you been recently?

    A. I spent the vacation with my family.

    B. There are 10 people.

    C. Where is it?

（B）18. Remember to turn off the light when you leave.

    A. Do not worry about my test.

    B. Don't worry. I will do it.

    C. Don't you remember my name?

（B）19. Hello! May I talk to Melody, please?

    A. I like Melody.

    B. She is not in.

    C. Melody is a sweet girl.

（C）20. It seems like it's going to rain soon.

    A. I will drink more water.

    B. Will you get a cold?

    C. I will bring my umbrella.

【單字】soon (adv.) 不久之後、很快地

【片語】get a cold = have a clod = catch a clod 感冒

第三部分：簡短對話聽力詳述解答

（B）21. **Man:** I love the ocean. It's so beautiful. But the beach is so crowded here.

Woman: There are so many people in the change room. You need to get in line and wait for a while.

Man: It is a long weekend. So just be patient and relax.

Question: What are they doing?

A. They are dancing.

B. They are on vacation.

C. They are buying clothing.

【單字】change room 更衣室
a while 一陣子
patient (adj.) 耐心的
relax (v.) 放輕鬆

（B）22. **Woman:** Oh, no. The elevator is broken! I think it's stuck between floors. There is no way out!

Man: Don't panic. I'll press the emergency button.

Question: What happened to them?

A. They are stuck in a traffic jam.

B. They are stuck in the elevator.

C. They are stuck in the mud.

【單字】 stuck (adj.) 卡住了
　　　　floor (n.) 樓層
　　　　panic (n.) (v.) 驚慌
　　　　emergency button (n.) 緊急按鈕
　　　　traffic jam 交通阻塞
　　　　elevator (n.) 電梯,指的是升降梯,英式用法則為 lift,而手
　　　　扶電梯為 escalator。
　　　　mud (n.) 泥濘

（B） 23. **Man:** It looks so good on you. Where did you buy the dress?

　　　　Woman: Oh! Thanks! I got it from the night market last night. It is brand new.

　　　　Man: Pink also looks gorgeous on you.

　　　　Question: What are they talking about?

　　　　A. A night market.

　　　　B. Clothing.

　　　　C. A brand of a car.

【單字】 dress (n.) 洋裝
　　　　brand (n.) 本為廠牌、名牌之意,但 brand new 二字為形容
　　　　詞,表示嶄新的、全新的。

【片語】 衣物 look+ { good / beautiful / gorgeous } + on 某人 = 指這件衣服穿在某人身上很漂亮

(A) 24.**Man:** Add some salt and... pepper. You know I love spicy food.

Woman: Can I put in some garlic? Are you afraid of its smell? After cooking, it won't be so strong. Garlic can prevent us from getting a cold. I am going to put some in now, OK?

Man: Wait! Oh..., too much!

Question: Where are they?

A. They are in a kitchen.

B. They are in a supermarket.

C. They are in a clinic.

【單字】spicy (adj.) 辛辣的

garlic (n.) 大蒜

【片語】prevent...from... 阻止／防止……免於……

(C) 25.**Woman:** Tom, are you in your room? Tom? Oh, here you are. Why didn't you answer me when I was calling you? Are you well?

Man: I am OK. Sorry. I'm in an awful mood and I just want to be alone.

Question: What is wrong with the man?

A. He feels sick.

B. He can not hear.

C. He feels down.

【片語】in a good mood 心情或情緒好

in a bad mood 心情或情緒壞

【單字】awful = bad，相反詞為 good = happy

down 當形容詞使用時的用法，在口語中十分普遍，就是 sad（難過）的意思。

（C）26. **Man:** Mom, what is for breakfast today?

Woman: Umm..., as usual, we are going to have some cereal with milk.

Man: Oh, I am sick of that.

Question: What is true according to the boy?

A. He loves eating breakfast every day.

B. He is sick and he doesn't feel hungry.

C. He doesn't like eating cereal with milk.

【單字】cereal (n.) 麥片粥

【片語】as usual (adv 片語) 與往常一樣地

be sick of... 厭倦或膩煩某人或某事

（B）27. **Woman:** You look so tired. What happened?

Man: Oh, do I? I stayed up until three o'clock in the morning.

Question: Why does the man look so tired?

A. He fixed the clock in the morning.

B. He didn't sleep until three o'clock in the morning.

C. He didn't eat anything in the morning.

【片語】stay up = sit up 熬夜

　　　　not...until / till... 直到……才……

(C) 28. **Man:** I think we'd better get rid of the map and ask for directions.

Woman: Good idea. The map is too old. We should ask someone for help or we won't get there on time.

Question: What happened to them?

A. They are mad.

B. They want to buy a map.

C. They are lost.

【單字】direction (n.) 方向

　　　　map (n.) 地圖

【片語】ask for directions 問路

　　　　某人'd better(助動詞) + 原形 V...
　　　　= 某人 had better(助動詞) + 原形 V...　} 某人最好……

　　　　get rid of... (v.) 除去……；擺脫……

　　　　get lost = be lost 迷路

(C) 29. **Man:** The Olympic Games are so amazing. Every runner is the best in his country. Wow! He is running so fast. The first one now is American. The one next to him is Number 10.

Woman: Number 10 is from China. How about Taiwan's runner?

Man: There he is! It seems impossible for him to get the medal.

Woman: Where? Number 5?

Question: What are the man and the woman doing?

A. They are going jogging.

B. They are traveling in China.

C. They are watching a TV program.

【單字】Olympic Games (n.) 奧林匹克運動會、世運會
medal (n.) 獎章
延伸單字： gold medal 金牌
　　　　　 silver medal 銀牌
　　　　　 bronze medal 銅牌

(C) 30. **Man:** Jenny broke up with her boy friend. She is feeling so bad.

Woman: Did you try to comfort her?

Man: She doesn't want to talk to anybody now. She told us to leave her alone.

Woman: Yes, I think it's better to leave her alone now.
Let's go for lunch.

Question: What are they about to do next?

A. They are about to break up.

B. They are about to talk to Jenny next.

C. They are about to go out for lunch.

【句型】 break up with ＋ 某人 ，與某人分手或決裂
leave ＋ 某人 ＋ alone ，避免打擾某人
be about to ＋ 原 V ，正即將……

重點筆記

本測驗分三部份，全部都是單選題，共30題，作答時間約20分鐘。作答說明為中文，印在試題冊上並經由錄音播出。

第一部分：看圖辨義

共10題，每題請聽錄音播出題目和三個英文句子之後，選出與所看到的圖畫最相符的答案。每題只播出一遍。

A

B

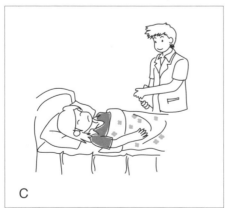

C

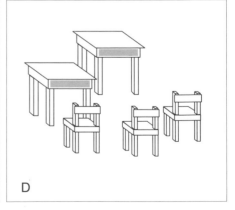

D

E

F

Helen's classes after school				
Mon	Tue	Wed	Thu	Fri
Math	English	Piano	Math	English

G

Welcome to Friday Restaurant

Open on weekdays:
11:00am~10:00pm

Open on weekends:
10:00am~11:00pm

H

I

考題請翻下一頁 ▶

第二部分：問答

共 10 題，每題請聽錄音播出的英文句子，再從試題冊上三個回答中，選出一個最適合的答案。每題只播出一遍。

11. A. Chocolate.

    B. History.

    C. I like noodles best.

12. A. In the park.

    B. Every morning.

    C. Last year.

13. A. We are on the earth.

    B. We are mowing the lawn.

    C. Are you kidding?

14. A. Fasten your seat belt, please.

    B. Be seated, please.

    C. Sorry, I didn't know it was taken.

15. A. I wear shoes.

    B. I will throw them away.

    C. I will. Don't worry.

16. A. How come! I fed him just now.

    B. We are hungry.

C. I just had it for lunch.

17. A. I have a cold.

B. I feel cold.

C. Put it through.

18. A. I like reading.

B. I prefer playing the guitar to the piano.

C. I like playing baseball and basketball.

19. A. Yes, here you are.

B. Close your eyes.

C. The library is closed.

20. A. You need to see the dentist.

B. I am going to brush your teeth.

C. How many teeth do you have?

第三部分：簡短對話

共10題，每題請聽錄音播出一段對話和一個相關的問題後，再從試題冊上三個選項中，選出一個最適合的答案。每段對話和問題播出<u>兩遍</u>。

21. A. She had an accident.

B. She was sick.

C. She studied too late last night.

22. A. No, she doesn't.

    B. Yes, she wants to go alone.

    C. Yes, she does.

23. A. She wants him to do his homework.

    B. She wants him to wash the dishes.

    C. She doesn't want him to do anything.

24. A. The woman's cousin.

    B. The man's cousin.

    C. Neither of them knows her.

25. A. She watched TV all the time.

    B. She played computer games all the time.

    C. She went out.

26. A. There is a telephone call from Wendy's friend.

    B. He wants Wendy to do the laundry.

    C. He wants to share the cake with Wendy.

27. A. A police station.

    B. A train station.

    C. A convenience store.

28. A. They need to prepare for the next test.

    B. The test was easy.

C. Both of them think they can pass the test.

29. A. In a post office.
    B. In the kitchen.
    C. In Tony's room.

30. A. They will keep waiting for the bus.
    B. The man will leave, and the woman will wait for the bus.
    C. The woman will get in the man's car.

第一部分：看圖辨義聽力詳述解答

（B） 1. For question 1, please look at picture A.

What is the boy doing?

A. He is reading a newspaper.

B. He is delivering newspapers.

C. He is delivering pizza.

【單字】deliver (v.) 投遞、遞送

（A） 2. For question 2, please look at picture B.

Where are they?

A. They are at the zoo.

B. They are in the restaurant.

C. They are in the classroom.

（A） 3. For question 3, please look at picture C.

How does the girl look?

A. She looks sick.

B. She looks excited.

C. She looks happy.

（B） 4. For question 4, please look at picture D.

How many desks and chairs do you see?

A. There are 3 desks and 2 chairs.

B. There are 2 desks and 3 chairs.

C. There are 5 chairs.

(A) 5. For question 5, please look at picture E.

Where are they?

A. They are in front of a church.

B. They are in a church.

C. They are in a supermarket.

(C) 6. For question 6, please look at picture F.

On what day does Helen have a piano lesson?

A. On Monday.

B. On Tuesday.

C. On Wednesday.

(A) 7. For question 7, please look at picture F again.

What class is on both Tuesday and Friday?

A. English.

B. Math.

C. Piano.

(C) 8. For question 8, please look at picture G.

What time does the restaurant open on Sundays?

A. 11 a.m.

B. 11 p.m.

C. 10 a.m.

(A) 9. For question 9, please look at picture H.

What are they doing?

A. They are celebrating the girl's birthday.

B. They are studying in a library.

C. They are brushing their teeth.

(A) 10. For question 10, please look at picture I.

What's happening?

A. The car has broken down.

B. The car is running.

C. The car has bumped into a building.

【片語】 run into = bump into 1.撞到；2.不期而遇

第二部分：問答聽力詳述解答

(B) 11. What subject do you like best?

A. Chocolate.

B. History.

C. I like noodles best.

【單字】 subject (n.) 科目

常見的科目： math (n.) 數學　　　　English (n.) 英文

history (n.) 歷史　　　geography (n.) 地理

science (n.) 自然科學　P.E. = physical education (n.) 體育

（B） 12. When do you go jogging?

　　　　A. In the park.

　　　　B. Every morning.

　　　　C. Last year.

（B） 13. What on earth are you doing, kids?

　　　　A. We are on the earth.

　　　　B. We are mowing the lawn.

　　　　C. Are you kidding?

【句型】on earth 放置 wh 疑問詞後，是表示「到底、究竟」
　　　　之意，與地球 earth 無關。

【單字】mow (v.) 割草、除草

　　　　lawn (n.) 草坪

（C） 14. Hey! That is my seat.

　　　　A. Fasten your seat belt, please.

　　　　B. Be seated, please.

　　　　C. Sorry, I didn't know it was taken.

【單字】sit (down) = be seated = seat oneself

（C） 15. Please take off your shoes.

　　　　A. I wear shoes.

B. I will throw them away.

C. I will. Don't worry.

【片語】take off 脫掉、起飛

(A) 16. Did you feed the dog? He seems hungry.

A. How come! I fed him just now.

B. We are hungry.

C. I just had it for lunch.

(C) 17. Mr. Chang, there is a call for you.

A. I have a cold.

B. I feel cold.

C. Put it through.

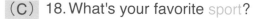

【解析】C 選項 put it through 的 it 表電話，put it through 表示 將電話轉接過來。

(C) 18. What's your favorite sport?

A. I like reading.

B. I prefer playing the guitar to the piano.

C. I like playing baseball and basketball.

【單字】favorite (n.) (adj.) 最喜愛 (的)

（A） 19. May I take a closer look at the T-shirt?

   A. Yes, here you are.

   B. Close your eyes.

   C. The library is closed.

【解析】closer 為 close 的比較級，「更靠近的」；A 選項中 Here you are.表示「你要的東西就在這裡」，當店員把東西拿給你看時可用這一句，所以答案是 A。

（A） 20. Mom, I have a toothache.

   A. You need to see the dentist.

   B. I am going to brush your teeth.

   C. How many teeth do you have?

【單字】toothache (n.) 牙痛

   dentist (n.) 牙醫

第三部分：簡短對話聽力詳述解答

（A） 21. **Man:** You are late for school today. Why?

   Woman: Because a car hit my bike this morning.

   Man: That's terrible. Are you alright?

   Question: Why is the student late for school?

   A. She had an accident.

B. She was sick.

C. She studied too late last night.

【單字】accident (n.) 意外事故

（C） 22. **Man:** Hello, Annie. Where are you going?

Woman: Hi, Tim. I am going to a movie.

Man: Really? Can I go with you?

Woman: Sure, why not?

Question: Does the woman want to go to a movie with the man?

A. No, she doesn't.

B. Yes, she wants to go alone.

C. Yes, she does.

【解析】why not? 表示「當然」之意，字面上 why not 即是「為何不要」、「哪有不要的道理」，所以聽到 why not 即是 Yes, of course. 之意！

（B） 23. **Woman:** Billy, did you finish your homework yet?

Man: No, Mom, I don't have any homework to do.

Woman: Then come help me do the dishes.

Question: What does the woman want Billy to do?

A. She wants him to do his homework.

B. She wants him to wash the dishes.

C. She doesn't want him to do anything.

名師解析

【片語】do the dishes = wash the dishes「洗碗盤」。現代人洗衣服（wash clothes）的方式，常是投入洗衣機再拿出來晾，這樣的工作英文用 do the laundry 表示。

(A) 24. **Man:** Do you know the girl standing in front of the bookstore?

Woman: Yes, she is Susan, my cousin.

Man: Could I have her phone number?

Question: Who is Susan?

A. The woman's cousin.

B. The man's cousin.

C. Neither of them knows her.

名師解析

【單字】cousin (n.) 表（堂）弟兄姊妹

C 選項中 neither 表示「兩者皆不、兩者皆非」。

(C) 25. **Woman:** How was your Chinese New Year vacation?

Man: Not too bad. I spent a lot of time watching TV and playing computer games.

Woman: Really? I hate watching TV. I would rather go out than stay at home whenever I have vacation.

Question: What did the woman probably do during Chinese New Year's vacation ?

A. She watched TV all the time.

B. She played computer games all the time.

C. She went out.

【句型】 would rather + 原形動詞A + than + 原形動詞B，寧願A而不要B。

【單字】 whenever (conj.) 無論何時

probably (adv.) 可能地

（C） 26. **Man:** Come here, Wendy!

Woman: Sorry, Dad, I am pretty busy right now.

Man: OK, then I will eat the cake all by myself.

Question: Why does Dad call Wendy?

A. There is a telephone call from Wendy's friend.

B. He wants Wendy to do the laundry.

C. He wants to share the cake with Wendy.

【單字】 by oneself = alone (adv.) 獨自地

【片語】 share...with 某人，與某人分享……

do the laundry 洗衣服

(B) 27. **Woman:** Excuse me, sir. Could you please tell me how to get to the train station?

Man: The train station? Well..., go straight and turn right at the Seven Eleven, and then go straight for two blocks. You won't miss it.

Woman: Thank you very much!

Question: Where will the woman go?

A. A police station.

B. A train station.

C. A convenience store.

【英文常識】block 可以是一種立體方塊、積木或障礙物。在美國市中心裏，一棟大的建築物似一方塊，所以走一街區（一大建築物體的路段），即稱為一個 block（街區）。

(A) 28. **Man:** The math test was so difficult. I don't think I will pass it.

Woman: Me, either. I think we had better study harder for the next test.

Man: Yeah. You can say that again.

Question: What do they mean?

A. They need to prepare for the next test.

B. The test was easy.

C. Both of them think they can pass the test.

【解析】肯定句後的「我也是」= Me, too.

否定句後的「我也是」= Me, either.

had better(助動詞)表示最好……，後面接原形動詞。

You can say that again. 表示認同他人先前所言，即「你說對了！」等於 Sure, of course.

(C) 29. **Woman:** Tony, it will become much colder tomorrow. Don't forget to wear a sweater.

Man: I know, Mom, but I can't find my sweater.

Woman: Let me see. It's right here at the bottom of your closet.

Question: Where are Tony and Mom?

A. In a post office.

B. In the kitchen.

C. In Tony's room.

【英文常識】 sweater (n.) 為毛衣，而 sweat (v.) (n.) 流汗，而可以聯想 sweat-er，為讓人流汗者，怪不得跟英國人比起來，美國人不喜歡穿毛衣。

【單字】 bottom (n.) 底部

at the bottom of...在……的底部

closet (n.) 衣櫥、壁櫥

(C) 30. **Man:** When will your bus arrive?

Woman: Maybe in ten minutes. I'm not sure.

Man: I think I can drive you home. Do you want a ride?

Woman: Yes! Thanks a lot! You are so kind.

Question: What are they going to do next?

A. They will keep waiting for the bus.

B. The man will leave, and the woman will wait for the bus.

C. The woman will get in the man's car.

【單字】maybe (adv.) = perhaps (adv.)

【片語】in+ 一段時 = 在……之後，立即……

【句型】男人問 Do you want a ride? = Do you need a lift? 那你需要搭我的便車嗎？

本測驗分三部份，全部都是單選題，共30題，作答時間約20分鐘。作答說明為中文，印在試題冊上並經由錄音播出。

第一部分：看圖辨義

共10題，每題請聽錄音播出題目和三個英文句子之後，選出與所看到的圖畫最相符的答案。每題只播出一遍。

A

B

C

D

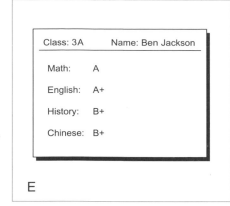

E

F

G

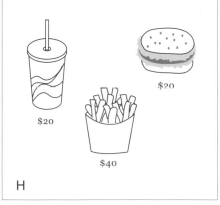

H

I

考題請翻下一頁 ▶

第二部分：問答

　　共 10 題，每題請聽錄音播出的英文句子，再從試題冊上三個回答中，選出一個最適合的答案。每題只播出**一遍**。

11. A. It doesn't matter.
　　 B. I don't know what is going on.
　　 C. The same to you.

12. A. I'll be glad to.
　　 B. You are not just saying.
　　 C. How could I say yes?

13. A. Where does it start?
　　 B. Let's go jogging.
　　 C. I think it is very likely.

14. A. You are welcome.
　　 B. Not at all.
　　 C. I will return it to you.

15. A. Thanks a lot.
　　 B. You can miss it.
　　 C. It's 0918282646.

16. A. I didn't read today's paper yet.
　　 B. Here you are.

C. But I like sugar.

17. A. What are you writing?

    B. No problem. Get in.

    C. Who is calling?

18. A. Sorry, I will be back with tea.

    B. I don't like tea, either.

    C. Coffee is healthier than tea.

19. A. I will buy water for you.

    B. Let's find a gas station.

    C. We got a ticket.

20. A. Well-done, please.

    B. I don't like steak.

    C. By taxi.

第三部分：簡短對話

共 10 題，每題請聽錄音播出一段對話和一個相關的問題後，再從試題冊上三個選項中，選出一個最適合的答案。每段對話和問題播出兩遍。

21. A. A taxi driver.

    B. A doctor.

    C. A baker.

22. A. She doesn't want to listen to the joke at all.

    B. She really likes to listen to the joke.

    C. She is taking a nap.

23. A. Have dinner with a friend.

    B. Buy a table.

    C. Make a reservation.

24. A. The woman doesn't know who Steve is.

    B. The woman is Steve's family.

    C. The woman is the man's friend.

25. A. She thinks that the man is funny.

    B. She doesn't believe he did not know about the party.

    C. She is going to invite him to a party.

26. A. Yes, he will take it. He likes it very much.

    B. No, he won't.

    C. He will take the English language course.

27. A. She can't find her book.

    B. She broke the glasses.

    C. She can't find her glasses.

28. A. Friends.

    B. Classmates.

C. Brother and sister.

29 A. Yes, she will.

B. No, she won't.

C. She hates to go because she doesn't like drinking coffee.

30. A. The bus station.

B. The post office.

C. The train station.

第一部分：看圖辨義聽力詳述解答

(B) 1. For question 1, please look at picture A.
   Which number is the fastest runner?
   A. Number 4.
   B. Number 15.
   C. Number 5.

(A) 2. For question 2, please look at picture B.
   Who is the heaviest?
   A. Andy.
   B. Kathy.
   C. Justin.

【單字】heavy (adj.) 重的
　　　　heaviest (adj.) 最重的

(C) 3. For question 3, please look at picture B again.
   Who is heavier than Kathy but lighter than Andy?
   A. Andy.
   B. Ken.
   C. Justin.

【單字】light (adj.) 輕的
　　　　lighter (adj.) 更輕的

（C） 4. For question 4, please look at picture C.

What is behind the woman?

A. A TV set is.

B. A knife is.

C. A refrigerator is.

【單字】behind... (prep.) 在……之後

refrigerator (n.) 電冰箱

（B） 5. For question 5, please look at picture D.

What is the boy doing?

A. He is watching a movie in a theater.

B. He is taking a shower.

C. He is shopping in a department store.

（B） 6. For question 6, please look at picture E.

What is true?

A. History is Ben's best subject.

B. Ben is best at English.

C. English is the worst subject for Ben.

【單字】best（最好的）為 good 的最高級，比較級為 better。

worst（最糟的）是 bad 的最高級。

good 好的→better 較好的→best 最好的

bad 糟的、壞的→worse 更糟的、更壞的→worst 最糟的、最壞的

(B) 7. For question 7, please look at picture F.

　　 What is the boy sitting on the bench doing?

　　 A. He is roller-blading.

　　 B. He is watching the other boy roller-blading.

　　 C. He is jumping.

【英文常識】bench (n.) 長椅，選項中的 roller-blading 為直排輪
　　　　　（運動），而其他類似滑動的運動有 roller-skating 雙排輪溜
　　　　　冰、ice-skating 冰上溜冰、skate boarding 滑板運動。

(C) 8. For question 8, please look at picture G.

　　 Where is the girl with straight long hair?

　　 A. On the left.

　　 B. On the right.

　　 C. In the middle.

【單字】straight (adj.) (adv.) 直的；直直地

(C) 9. For question 9, please look at picture H.

　　 If you buy a coke, a hamburger, and French fries, how
　　 much would you pay for all?

　　 A. 40 dollars.

　　 B. 20 dollars.

　　 C. 80 dollars.

（B） 10. For question 10, please look at picture I.

What does the man do?

A. He is a baker.

B. He is a farmer.

C. He is a firefighter.

【單字】baker (n.) 麵包師傅

firefighter (n.) 救火員

第二部分：問答聽力詳述解答

（C） 11. Have a nice day!

A. It doesn't matter.

B. I don't know what is going on.

C. The same to you.

【解析】Have a nice day! = Have a good day! 外國人不管在
何地，白天與人（甚至陌生人）道別時，除了 good-bye
外，亦可使用這句子。

【單字】matter (v.) 重大關係

【句型】the same to you 給你相同的祝福

（A） 12. Give my regards to your parents.

A. I'll be glad to.

B. You are not just saying.

C. How could I say yes?

【句型】give / send regards to ＋某人 = say hello to ＋某人，
向某人問候

（C） 13. I am afraid it is going to rain.

　　　　A. Where does it start?

　　　　B. Let's go jogging.

　　　　C. I think it is very likely.

（B） 14. I hope I am not disturbing you.

　　　　A. You are welcome.

　　　　B. Not at all.

　　　　C. I will return it to you.

【單字】disturb (v.) 打擾

（C） 15. What's your cell phone number, please?

　　　　A. Thanks a lot.

　　　　B. You can miss it.

　　　　C. It's 0918282646.

【單字】cell phone (n.) 手機、行動電話

（B） 16. Please pass me the pepper.

      A. I didn't read today's paper yet.

      B. Here you are.

      C. But I like sugar.

（B） 17. Can you give me a ride home?

      A. What are you writing?

      B. No problem. Get in.

      C. Who is calling?

【片語】give +某人 + a ride　給某人搭乘（任何交通工具）

（A） 18. I ordered a cup of tea, not a cup of coffee.

      A. Sorry, I will be back with tea.

      B. I don't like tea, either.

      C. Coffee is healthier than tea.

【單字】order (v.) (n.) 訂購；點餐

（B） 19. Oops, we have run out of oil.

      A. I will buy water for you.

      B. Let's find a gas station.

      C. We got a ticket.

【片語】run out of... 用光了……；用盡了……

（A）20. How would you like your steak?
   A. Well-done, please.
   B. I don't like steak.
   C. By taxi.

【英文常識】服務生會問顧客「牛排要幾分熟呢？」"How
   would you like your steak?" 然而吃完後服務生問「剛
   剛吃的牛排您還喜歡嗎？」則是 "How did you like your
   steak?" 注意兩個句子中的時態是不同，而前一句的
   would like＝want，而後句 did 出現於句中表過去式，客
   人已經吃過牛排了，問是否喜歡；而 how 表程度，所以
   後句表示問客人吃完牛排後，喜歡的程度為何？

第三部分：簡短對話聽力詳述解答

（B）21. **Man:** How do you feel today?
   Woman: I feel much better now, but I still cough a lot.
   Man: I see. I'll give you some medicine that will relieve
      your cough.
   Question: Who is the man?
   A. A taxi driver.
   B. A doctor.
   C. A baker.

【單字】relieve (v.) 緩和、減輕
   cough (v.) (n.) 咳嗽

（A） 22. **Man:** Hey, Dolly, I got another funny joke. Do you want to listen?

Dolly: Oh, come on! Give me a break! I am not available.

Question: What does Dolly mean?

A. She doesn't want to listen to the joke at all.

B. She really likes to listen to the joke.

C. She is taking a nap.

【單字】fun (adj.) 有趣的；(n.) 樂趣
　　　funny (adj.) 滑稽的、可笑的
　　　available (adj.) 可得的、有空的
【片語】Give me a break! 饒了我吧！
　　　take a nap 小憩

（A） 23. **Man:** May I help you, madam?

Woman: Yes, last night I made a reservation for a table for two under the name of Candy.

Man: Let me check. Madam, your table is number 8.

Question: What is the woman going to do?

A. Have dinner with a friend.

B. Buy a table.

C. Make a reservation.

【片語】make a reservation (v.) 預約

（A） 24. **Man:** Hello, may I speak to Steve?

Woman: Steve? I'm afraid that you must have the wrong number.

Man: I'm very sorry.

Question: What is true?

A. The woman doesn't know who Steve is.

B. The woman is Steve's family.

C. The woman is the man's friend.

【單字】 must (助動詞)，有時表示「必須」之意，而有時表示 推測「一定……」，在此表示「一定」之意。

（B） 25. **Woman:** Why didn't you come to our party last night?

Man: Your party? I didn't know about it at all.

Nobody told me.

Woman: You are kidding!

Question: What does the woman mean?

A. She thinks that the man is funny.

B. She doesn't believe he did not know about the party.

C. She is going to invite him to a party.

（B） 26. **Woman:** Do you like this class? I think it's very interesting.

Man: Well, I think maybe I should take another course.

Woman: Come on, you'll like it after learning about it.

Man: I don't think so. I don't like chemistry as much as you.

Question: Will the man take the chemistry course?

A. Yes, he will take it. He likes it very much.

B. No, he won't.

C. He will take the English language course.

名師解析

【單字】course 可以表示路程、課程、進程，甚至是一道菜。在此為課程，選修課程的動詞為 take。
chemistry (n.) 化學

【片語】come on 有二種意思，一為「來嘛！走嘛！」二為「少來了！」此處為「來嘛！」，表邀約一同之意。

(C) 27. **Woman:** Could you come to help me now?

Man: Sure, what happened?

Woman: I can't find my glasses, and I can't see anything.

Man: They're right on your head.

Question: Why does the woman call for help?

A. She can't find her book.

B. She broke the glasses.

C. She can't find her glasses.

名師解析

【單字】glass 可以是玻璃或玻璃杯，但當字尾加 es 為複數型態時，則可表示眼鏡。

（C） 28. **Woman:** What are Mom and Dad talking about?

Man: They are talking about hiring a tutor to teach you English.

Woman: Oh, no. They should have one to teach you first. My English is better than yours.

Question: What's the relationship between the boy and the girl?

A. Friends.

B. Classmates.

C. Brother and sister.

【單字】tutor (n.) (v.) 家教

relationship (n.) 關係

【解析】one 為不定代名詞，其意義要視上文而定，在此指「一位家教」。

（B） 29. **Man:** Let's take a break. How about going to the coffee shop and having a cup of coffee?

Woman: I would like to, but I haven't finished my work. I think I'll finish it first.

Question: Will the woman go to the coffee shop with the man right away?

A. Yes, she will.

B. No, she won't.

C. She hates to go because she doesn't like drinking coffee.

【片語】take a break 休息一下
【單字】right away = right off = at once = in no time = immediately
　　　　(adv.) 立刻地

（C）30. **Woman:** We should be there as soon as possible.

　　　　Man: Take your time. I'm not in a hurry.

　　　　Woman: But we have to get on the train on time!

　　　　Question: Where are they going?

　　　　A. The bus station.

　　　　B. The post office.

　　　　C. The train station.

【片語】as...as possible 盡可能地……
　　　　as soon as possible 盡快地
　　　　in a hurry 匆忙
　　　　get on 上車（指公共交通工具），其相反詞為get off（下車）

本測驗分三部份，全部都是單選題，共 30 題，作答時間約 20 分鐘。作答說明為中文，印在試題冊上並經由錄音播出。

第一部分：看圖辨義

共 10 題，每題請聽錄音播出題目和三個英文句子之後，選出與所看到的圖畫最相符的答案。每題只播出一遍。

A

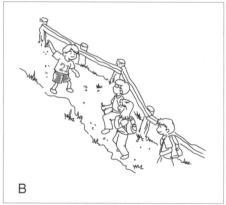

B

C

D

E

F

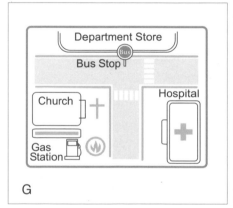

G

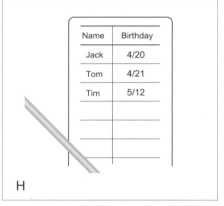

H

考題請翻下一頁 ▶

第二部分：問答

共 10 題，每題請聽錄音播出的英文句子，再從試題冊上三個回答中，選出一個最適合的答案。每題只播出一遍。

11. A. I've never eaten steak.
    B. My compliments to the chef.
    C. Don't ask me a silly question.

12. A. I am fine.
    B. It is fine.
    C. No, not yet.

13. A. It is very nice.
    B. Around eight-thirty.
    C. For about a week.

14. A. I don't like hot dogs.
    B. Under the bench at the playground.
    C. The dog is funny.

15. A. I usually go to school by bus.
    B. At my grandma's house.
    C. I like my school very much.

16. A. I always like to be late.
    B. Sorry, because of the heavy traffic.

C. I have been fine lately.

17. A. Let me turn off the air conditioner.

B. I will give you iced water soon.

C. I had a cold.

18. A. No, I will have a watch.

B. OK, I won't.

C. OK, I will.

19. A. He is from Korea.

B. He can speak Japanese.

C. He has no money.

20. A. I lost my bike yesterday.

B. I had a car accident.

C. The legs of the desk are broken.

第三部分：簡短對話

　　共10題，每題請聽錄音播出一段對話和一個相關的問題後，再從試題冊上三個選項中，選出一個最適合的答案。每段對話和問題播出兩遍。

21. A. Water.

B. Coke.

C. Juice.

22. A. He will leave a message.
    B. He will call back.
    C. He will buy a telephone.

23. A. After dinner.
    B. Before dinner.
    C. Before lunch.

24. A. Chicken burger.
    B. Ice cream.
    C. Cheese burger.

25. A. In a warm place.
    B. On board an airplane.
    C. In Alaska, a cold place.

26. A. She is hungry.
    B. She is sick.
    C. She looks well.

27. A. They got mad.
    B. They got lost.
    C. They got arrested in the police office.

28. A. She is in Tainan.
    B. Nobody knows.

C. She is in Taipei.

29. A. He doesn't like Mary.
    B. He has a midterm exam.
    C. He feels bad.

30. A. They will watch a musical.
    B. They will buy a watch.
    C. They will watch birds.

第一部分：看圖辨義聽力詳述解答

(C) 1. For question 1, please look at picture A.

What are they doing?

A. They are walking along the street.

B. They are jumping rope.

C. They are jogging.

【單字】along (prep.) 沿著、順著

jump rope 跳繩

jog (v.) 慢跑

(B) 2. For question 2, please look at picture B.

Where are they?

A. They are on a beach.

B. They are on a hill.

C. They are beside a hospital.

【單字】hill (n.) 小山丘

beside (prep.) 在……旁邊

(C) 3. For question 3, please look at picture C.

What does he do?

A. He is a florist.

B. He is a secretary.

C. He is a firefighter.

【單字】florist (n.) 花店主人、賣花的人
　　　　secretary (n.) 秘書

（B） 4. For question 4, please look at picture D.
　　　 What does the sign mean?
　　　 A. Do not take a bath in a bathtub.
　　　 B. Do not swim in the river.
　　　 C. Do not drink the water from the river.

【單字】sign (n.) 看牌、號誌、標示
　　　　bathtub (n.) 浴缸
【片語】take a bath (v.) 洗澡

（C） 5. For question 5, please look at picture E.
　　　 What can you not do here?
　　　 A. Study math.
　　　 B. Read a magazine.
　　　 C. Shout aloud.

【單字】aloud (adv.) 大聲地

（B） 6. For question 6, please look at picture F.

What is it?

A. It is a map.

B. It is a menu.

C. It is a timetable.

【單字】map (n.) 地圖

menu (n.) 菜單

timetable (n.) 時刻表

（A） 7. For question 7, please look at picture F again.

If you are thirsty, you are going to order pearl milk tea.

How much do you have to pay?

A. 30 dollars.

B. 140 dollars.

C. 40 dollars.

【英文常識】pearl milk tea 珍珠奶茶，pearl 是珍珠的意思，

還記得一部電影叫珍珠港（Pearl Harbor）嗎？

（A） 8. For question 8, please look at picture G.

Where is the bus stop?

A. In front of the department store.

B. In front of the gas station.

C. Between the church and the gas station.

【單字】gas 汽油為 gasoline 的簡稱。

（B）9. For question 9, please look at picture G again.

Where is the church?

A. Across from the gas station.

B. Across from the hospital.

C. Next to the department store.

（B）10. For question 10, please look at picture H.

When is Tom's birthday?

A. April 20th.

B. April 21st.

C. May 2nd.

【英文常識】日期需用序數，1st = first，2nd = second，3rd = third，4th = fourth...等，所以 4 月 20 日 April 20th，而 4 月 21 日 April 21st（唸成 twenty-first），而 22 日（唸成 twenty-second）。

第二部分：問答聽力詳述解答

（B）11. How did you like your steak?

A. I've never eaten steak.

B. My compliments to the chef.

C. Don't ask me a silly question.

【解析】服務生問客人喜不喜歡牛排，客人通常不是抱怨就是
　　　　讚美，而 B 選項表示在吃完餐點後，客人向服務生稱讚廚師
　　　　很會做菜之意。

【單字】compliment (v.) 稱讚；(n.) 讚美的話
　　　　chef (n.) 主廚、大師傅

（B） 12. How is the weather today?

A. I am fine.

B. It is fine.

C. No, not yet.

（B） 13. What time is it?

A. It is very nice.

B. Around eight- thirty.

C. For about a week.

（B） 14. Where did you find the dog?

A. I don't like hot dogs.

B. Under the bench at the playground.

C. The dog is funny.

【單字】bench (n.) 長板凳
　　　　playground (n.) 操場、兒童遊樂場

141

（A）15. How do you go to school?

    A. I usually go to school by bus.

    B. At my grandma's house.

    C. I like my school very much.

（B）16. Why are you so late?

    A. I always like to be late.

    B. Sorry, because of the heavy traffic.

    C. I have been fine lately.

（A）17. I feel so cold.

    A. Let me turn off the air conditioner.

    B. I will give you iced water soon.

    C. I had a cold.

（B）18. Don't watch TV anymore.

    A. No, I will have a watch.

    B. OK, I won't.

    C. OK, I will.

 名師解析

【解析】當對方要求 Don't...（不要……）時，回答有2種：

OK = No, I won't.（好啦！我不會這麼做。）這裡的 no 譯為「好啦。」因為對方要求不要做某一件事，所以回應 no 表示不會做這件事，附和對方所求。

而若對方要求 Don't...（不要……），而你無法或不願配合，則可回答 Sorry, I will.（對不起，我要這麼做。）

(A) 19. Where does he come from?

   A. He is from Korea.

   B. He can speak Japanese.

   C. He has no money.

(B) 20. What's wrong with your leg?

   A. I lost my bike yesterday.

   B. I had a car accident.

   C. The legs of the desk are broken.

【單字】accident 意外；車禍

第三部分：簡短對話聽力詳述解答

(C) 21. **Woman:** I am so thirsty. Do you have anything to drink?

   Man: There is some juice, cold water and milk in the refrigerator. What would you like?

   Woman: Juice would be great. Thank you.

   Question: What does the woman want to drink?

   A. Water.

   B. Coke.

   C. Juice.

(B) 22. **Man:** Hello, may I speak to Melody?

   Woman: She is not here.

Man: When will she be back?

Woman: I don't know. Would you like to leave a message?

Man: No, Thanks. I will phone back.

Question: What will the man do later?

A. He will leave a message.

B. He will call back.

C. He will buy a telephone.

【單字】打電話的動詞可以是 call = telephone = phone = make a call

(A) 23. **Boy:** Mommy, Uncle Joe gave me some sweet chocolate. Can I eat it now?

Woman: No! Dinner is almost ready.

Boy: Oh, no! When can I eat it?

Woman: After we have had dinner.

Question: When can the kid eat chocolate?

A. After dinner.

B. Before dinner.

C. Before lunch.

(C) 24. **Woman:** Welcome. May I take your order?

Man: Yes, I would like one cheese burger and a cup of coffee.

Woman: For here or to go?

Man: For here.

Question: What does the man order?

A. Chicken burger.

B. Ice cream.

C. Cheese burger.

【解析】waiter（服務生）或 waitress（女服務生），常問客人，可以點菜了嗎，就是 May I take your order?

fast food restaurant（速食店）的 cashier（櫃檯的收銀員），常問客人 for here or to go?（這裏吃或外帶？）

(C) 25. **Man:** Welcome to Alaska.

Woman: Oooo...,it's so cold here.

Man: It's a whole new experience, isn't it?

Woman: Yes, my country is very warm. I have never been to such a cold place.

Man: You will have fun! Enjoy your trip!

Question: Where does the conversation take place?

A. In a warm place.

B. On board an airplane.

C. In Alaska, a cold place.

【片語】a whole new experience 全新的經驗

take place (v.) = happen 發生

on board 在飛機上或船上

（B）26. **Man:** Nancy, what's wrong with you? You don't look well.

　　Woman: I don't feel well. I have a stomachache.

　　Man: Do you want to see a doctor?

　　Woman: I think so. Can you take me to the doctor?

　　Question: What's wrong with Nancy?

　　A. She is hungry.

　　B. She is sick.

　　C. She looks well.

（B）27. **Man:** I have totally lost my way. Where are we now?

　　Woman: I don't know, either.

　　Man: The policeman is right here. Let's ask him for help.

　　Woman: That's a great idea.

　　Question: What happened to these two people?

　　A. They got mad.

　　B. They got lost.

　　C. They got arrested in the police office.

【單字】mad (adj.) = angry (adj.) 生氣的

【片語】be / get lost 迷路

　　　be / get arrested 被逮捕

（C）28. **Man:** Where is Melody?

　　Woman: She has gone to Taipei on business.

　　Man: When will she come back?

　　Woman: In 2 days.

Question: Where is Melody now?

A. She is in Tainan.

B. Nobody knows.

C. She is in Taipei.

【片語】has gone to...已經去……

on business 出差，而 business 這個字為生意、事情、事業……之意。

【解析】in 2 days 表示 2 天之後立即回來，in + 一段時間 = 表示……之後，即……

（B） 29. **Woman:** Peter, Mary is giving a party tonight. Do you want to go?

Man: No. I need to prepare for my midterm exam.

Woman: That's too bad. It will be a great party.

Question: Why does Peter not join Mary's party?

A. He doesn't like Mary.

B. He has a midterm exam.

C. He feels bad.

【單字】辦舞會（餐會）的動詞可以是 give = have = throw = host，而 party 是舞會也可以是餐會、聚會，不一定是要跳舞，現代用語即為派對。

midterm exam (n.) 期中考試

mid 表 the middle of 中間的、中央的

term 期；期限、學期，所以 midterm exam 為期中考試

(A) 30. **Man:** Sara, do you have any plans for New Year's Eve?

Woman: Mary and I are going to watch a musical downtown.

Man: Sounds great.

Woman: Do you want to join us?

Man: I would love to.

Question: What will the speakers likely do on New Year Eve?

A. They will watch a musical.

B. They will buy a watch.

C. They will watch birds.

【單字】music (n.) 音樂

musical (adj.) 音樂的，(n.) 歌舞劇

downtown (n.) 市中心、鬧區

本測驗分三部份，全部都是單選題，共30題，作答時間約20分鐘。作答說明為中文，印在試題冊上並經由錄音播出。

第一部分：看圖辨義

共10題，每題請聽錄音播出題目和三個英文句子之後，選出與所看到的圖畫最相符的答案。每題只播出一遍。

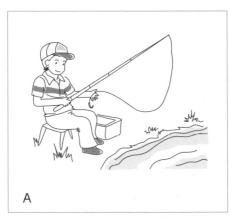

A

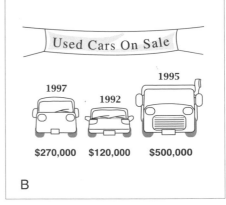

B

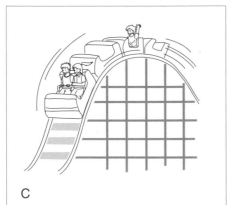

C

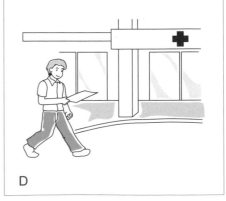

D

E

F

G

H

考題請翻下一頁 ▶

第二部分：問答

共10題，每題請聽錄音播出的英文句子，再從試題冊上三個回答中，選出一個最適合的答案。每題只播出一遍。

11. A. I am hungry.

    B. Because it is a rainy day.

    C. I got sick.

12. A. What a pity!

    B. I am proud of you.

    C. Oh, you are a second grader now.

13. A. Pretty good! How about you?

    B. I haven't seen John, either.

    C. I am too tired to take a walk.

14. A. I speak English well.

    B. Well-done.

    C. I have a headache.

15. A. Yes, please.

    B. Yes, I don't like milk.

    C. No, I like coffee very much.

16. A. It is very helpful.

    B. No, thanks!

C. It is my pleasure.

17. A. Well, let me slow down a little bit.

    B. I cannot catch up with you.

    C. I caught a cold, too.

18. A. I was born in 1986.

    B. I was born in Taiwan.

    C. My birthday is January 1ˢᵗ.

19. A. Sure, here you go.

    B. Yes, I will give you my pen.

    C. Are you thirsty?

20. A. Bury it now.

    B. Don't cry.

    C. No wonder the walkman is not working.

第三部分：簡短對話

共 10 題，每題請聽錄音播出一段對話和一個相關的問題後，再從試題冊上三個選項中，選出一個最適合的答案。每段對話和問題播出<u>兩遍</u>。

21. A. He has taught English for 13 years.

    B. He is a new English teacher.

    C. He will retire this June.

22. A. Do nothing.

    B. Buy vegetables and beef.

    C. Wait for Betty at the supermarket.

23. A. She doesn't like the red one.

    B. The size of the red one is too small.

    C. The size of the red one is too big.

24. A. By bicycle.

    B. On foot.

    C. By motorcycle.

25. A. She will eat breakfast at home.

    B. She will eat breakfast at school.

    C. She will not eat any breakfast.

26. A. Paid attention in class and reviewed.

    B. Took a nap in class.

    C. Talked to other classmates.

27. A. In a bathroom.

    B. At a zoo.

    C. At the crossroad.

28. A. In 15 minutes.

    B. In 30 minutes.

C. In 10 minutes.

29. A. 1 day.
    B. 2 days.
    C. 3 days.

30. A. At 7 a.m.
    B. At 7 p.m.
    C. At midnight.

第一部分：看圖辨義聽力詳述解答

(C) 1. For question 1, please look at picture A.

　　 What is the man doing?

　　 A. He is mountain climbing.

　　 B. He is exercising.

　　 C. He is fishing.

【英文常識】 mountain climbing 雖然和 hiking 的中文皆為爬
　　　　　　 山，但二種是不同的運動，climb 是指用手腳攀爬的
　　　　　　 爬，而 hiking 是徒步登山。mountain climbing 需要高度
　　　　　　 的技術及較好的體能。

【單字】 exercise (n.) (v.) 運動
　　　　 fish (n.) 魚， (v.) 釣魚

(C) 2. For question 2, please look at picture B.

　　 How old is the truck?

　　 A. It was made in 1997.

　　 B. It was made in 1992.

　　 C. It was made in 1995.

【句型】 How old...可以問人的年齡或車齡或屋齡……等，用
　　　　 法很廣。

(A) 3. For question 3, please look at picture B again.

155

How much is the car made in 1992?

A. $ 120,000.

B. $ 270,000.

C. $ 500,000.

(C) 4. For question 4, please look at picture C.

What are they riding?

A. They are riding a bike.

B. They are riding a horse.

C. They are riding a roller coaster.

【單字】roller coaster (n.) 雲霄飛車

(B) 5. For question 5, please look at picture C again.

Where are they?

A. In a museum.

B. In an amusement park.

C. In a music room.

【單字】museum (n.) 博物館

amusement park (n.) 遊樂園

music room (n.) 音樂教室

(C) 6. For question 6, please look at picture D.

Where is the man going?

A. He is going shopping.

B. He is going to an art museum.

C. He is going to a hospital.

【單字】art museum (n.) 美術館

(B) 7. For question 7, please look at picture E.

What is true?

A. The rabbit wins.

B. The turtle wins.

C. A turtle can hop faster than a rabbit.

【解析】hop 為跳、躍，青蛙(frog)及兔子(rabbit)會做 hop（跳）的動作，而 turtle（烏龜）不可能會 hop。

(C) 8. For question 8, please look at picture F.

What is he doing?

A. He is boating.

B. He is smoking.

C. He is hiking.

【單字】boat 為小船，此處當動詞則為划船或乘船遊玩。

157

（C）9. For question 9, please look at picture G.

Where is the girl coming from?

A. From a police station.

B. From a school.

C. From a convenience store.

【單字】便利商店是 convenience store，注意不是 convenient store。

（B）10. For question 10, please look at picture H.

What is the boy doing?

A. He is turning off the light.

B. He is sleeping.

C. He is making the bed.

【片語】turn off 關閉

make the bed 整理床鋪

第二部分：問答聽力詳述解答

（C）11. Why didn't you go to school?

A. I am hungry.

B. Because it is a rainy day.

C. I got sick.

(B) 12. Mom, I got a good grade in math.

    A. What a pity!

    B. I am proud of you.

    C. Oh, you are a second grader now.

【單字】grade 可以指成績、年級，聽力所聽到的 good grade
= high grade，指的是好成績，而 C 選項中的 grader 為……
年級的學生，second grader 即是指二年級的學生。

【句型】What a pity! 好可惜！
feel / be proud of + 某人；表示以某人為榮。

(A) 13. Long time no see. How have you been?

    A. Pretty good! How about you?

    B. I haven't seen John, either.

    C. I am too tired to take a walk.

【句型】How have you been? 與 How are you? 都是類似的意
思，即表示問候，二句只有時態上的不同而已。

(C) 14. You don't look well.

    A. I speak English well.

    B. Well-done.

    C. I have a headache.

【解析】這句子的 well 是形容詞，You don't look well.表示你
看起來好像身體不舒服的樣子。well-done 可以表示「做得
很棒！做得很好！」或「牛排全熟」的意思。

(A) 15. Would you like coffee with milk?

A. Yes, please.

B. Yes, I don't like milk.

C. No, I like coffee very much.

(C) 16. Thanks for your help.

A. It is very helpful.

B. No, thanks!

C. It is my pleasure.

(A) 17. I can not catch what you say.

A. Well, let me slow down a little bit.

B. I cannot catch up with you.

C. I caught a cold, too.

【單字】catch (v.) 抓住、趕上或說不清楚時，當對方說太快
時，你可以說 I cannot catch what you say.（我聽不清楚你
所說的）。

(B) 18. Where were you born?

A. I was born in 1986.

B. I was born in Taiwan.

C. My birthday is January 1ˢᵗ.

(A) 19. May I borrow your eraser, please?

A. Sure, here you go.

B. Yes, I will give you my pen.

C. Are you thirsty?

【單字】eraser (n.) 橡皮擦、板擦

(C) 20. The battery is dead.

A. Bury it now.

B. Don't cry.

C. No wonder the walkman is not working.

【單字】dead (adj.) 死亡的

battery (n.) 電池。電池沒電可以用 dead 表示，而電池快沒電了則可用 low 表示。

第三部分：簡短對話聽力詳述解答

(C) 21. **Man:** How many years has Mr. Watson taught English in our school?

Woman: By the time he retires this June, he will have taught English for 30 years.

Man: Wow! He is the most experienced teacher in our school.

Woman: You can say that again.

Question: What is true about Mr. Watson?

A. He has taught English for 13 years.

B. He is a new English teacher.

C. He will retire this June.

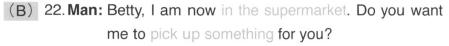

【單字】experienced (adj.) 有經驗的

　　　retire (v.) 退休

【句型】You can say that again. 表「你說得對，我也認同。」

(B) 22. **Man:** Betty, I am now in the supermarket. Do you want me to pick up something for you?

Woman: It is so nice of you. Well..., could you get some fresh vegetables and beef? I want to make dinner for all of you.

Man: Really? I cannot wait.

Question: What is the man going to do after the conversation?

A. Do nothing.

B. Buy vegetables and beef.

C. Wait for Betty at the supermarket.

【單字】 vegetable (n.) 蔬菜

beef (n.) 牛肉

cannot wait 表示迫不及待

(C) 23. **Woman:** You look great in this red T-shirt.

Man: Thank you. Do you have a smaller one? This one is too big.

Woman: Why don't you try this blue one?

Question: Why does the woman ask the man to try another one?

A. She doesn't like the red one.

B. The size of the red one is too small.

C. The size of the red one is too big.

【解析】 這裏的 one 皆是文中所指的 T-shirt。

【單字】 size (n.) 尺寸、大小

(A) 24. **Woman:** Josh, how do you go to school everyday?

Man: I go to school by bicycle.

Woman: Me, too.

Question: How do they go to school?

A. By bicycle.

B. On foot.

C. By motorcycle.

【句型】by + 交通工具，但徒步為 on foot。

（B） 25. **Man:** Joyce, go downstairs and have breakfast.

Woman: Dad, I can't. I am going to be late for school.

Man: No way. Breakfast is the most important meal of the day.

Woman: I will take it with me. Bye!

Question: What will Joyce probably do with her breakfast?

A. She will eat breakfast at home.

B. She will eat breakfast at school.

C. She will not eat any breakfast.

【單字】meal (n.) 三餐中任何一餐

　　　probably (adv.) 可能地

（A） 26. **Man:** Nancy, you got excellent grades on your final exam.

Woman: Thank you.

Man: How did you do that?

Woman: I just took notes in my class and reviewed them twice after class.

Question: How did Nancy do well on her final exam?

A. Paid attention in class and reviewed.

B. Took a nap in class.

C. Talked to other classmates.

【單字】excellent (adj.) 極佳的、優秀的

final exam (n.) 期末考

review (n.) (v.) 複習

twice (n.) 二次

【片語】take a note = take notes (v.) 作筆記

after class 下課後

（B）27. **Boy:** Mommy, do you see that funny monkey shaking its head?

Woman: No, which one?

Boy: It is in the corner. It is shaking its head.

Woman: Where? Oh, now I see it. Look! Another monkey is scratching its back.

Question: Where does the conversation take place?

A. In a bathroom.

B. At a zoo.

C. At the crossroad.

【單字】shake (v.) 搖、晃

corner (n.) 角落

scratch (v.) 抓

crossroad = intersection 十字路口

（C） 28. **Woman:** May I help you?

Man: Yes, could you tell me which bus goes to Chiang Kai-shek Memorial Hall?

Woman: The Number 15 bus goes to Chiang Kai-shek Memorial every 30 minutes and it will arrive in about 10 minutes.

Man: Thank you.

Question: When will the bus arrive?

A. In 15 minutes.

B. In 30 minutes.

C. In 10 minutes.

【單字】Chiang Kai-shek Memorial Hall (n.) 中正紀念館是台北重要的地標(landmark)

memorial (n.) 可以是紀念物、紀念碑、紀念館……等之意。

arrive (v.) 到達

【句型】every 30 minutes 每隔30分鐘，every + 數字 + 時間單位 = 每隔……

（B） 29. **Man:** Hello, this is Great Hotel. May I help you?

Woman: Yes, I want to book a double room for this coming Thursday and Friday.

Man: May I have your name please?

Woman: Joy Lin.

Question: How many days will the woman make a reservation for?

A. 1 day.

B. 2 days.

C. 3 days.

【單字】double room (n.) 雙人房

【片語】make a reservation 預約

(B) 30. **Woman:** Emperor Restaurant. May I help you?

Man: Yes, I'd like to make a reservation for this evening.

Woman: What time will you arrive?

Man: About seven o'clock.

Question: When will they arrive at the restaurant?

A. At 7 a.m.

B. At 7 p.m.

C. At midnight.

【單字】emperor (n.) 帝王

midnight (n.) 深夜

【解析】 arrive $\begin{cases} \boxed{in} + 大地方 \\ \boxed{at} + 小地方 \end{cases}$

本測驗分三部份，全部都是單選題，共30題，作答時間約20分鐘。作答說明為中文，印在試題冊上並經由錄音播出。

第一部分：看圖辨義

共10題，每題請聽錄音播出題目和三個英文句子之後，選出與所看到的圖畫最相符的答案。每題只播出一遍。

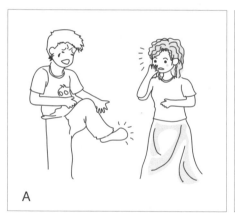

A

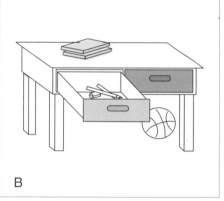

B

Trip to Kenting	
Bus to Kenting	$350
Bus back to Taichung	$350
Hotel for 1 night	$500
Food for 1 day	$200

C

D

Michelle Cart
173 Main Avenue,
Los Angeles, CA 90722-3407

Mr. Charles Chen

4F 220, Chung Shan Road,
Taipei City, 105 Taiwan

E

F

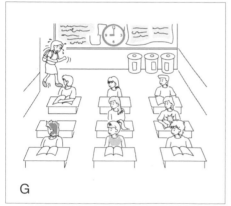

G

H

I

考題請翻下一頁 ▶

第二部分：問答

共10題，每題請聽錄音播出的英文句子，再從試題冊上三個回答中，選出一個最適合的答案。每題只播出一遍。

11. A. I am 17 years old.
    B. I am fine. How about you?
    C. I am from Canada.

12. A. It is, isn't it?
    B. Your dream will come true.
    C. Wow, it is so delicious.

13. A. Pretty good, and you?
    B. I am serious.
    C. Sure, go ahead.

14. A. How do you do?
    B. He is not busy now.
    C. He is a dentist.

15. A. Yes, I won't be the last one.
    B. OK. I will know soon.
    C. Lin, L-I-N.

16. A. Yes, I did.
    B. No, I am on vacation now.

C. Thanks. I am not hungry now.

17. A. I will help you with the homework later.

B. Yes, I am looking for a necktie for my husband.

C. No, I am going to help you.

18. A. She is not home.

B. Jean is a good friend.

C. Let's have a talk.

19. A. For many years.

B. Every 20 minutes.

C. Come on! Let's go have fun.

20. A. Yes, he did.

B. No, he won't.

C. In a couple of hours.

第三部分：簡短對話

共 10 題，每題請聽錄音播出一段對話和一個相關的問題後，再從試題冊上三個選項中，選出一個最適合的答案。每段對話和問題播出<u>兩遍</u>。

21. A. The woman really needs to be on a diet.

B. The man wants the woman to lose some weight.

C. The woman doesn't look fat.

22. A. The movie was terrific.
    B. He did not watch all of the movie.
    C. He enjoyed the movie very much.

23. A. It's 4:30.
    B. It's 2:40.
    C. It's 3:40.

24. A. The man will call the woman in the early morning.
    B. The woman doesn't like the man.
    C. The woman goes to bed late.

25. A. She is sleeping.
    B. She is studying.
    C. She is watching TV.

26. A. She is going to close the window.
    B. She is going to open the window.
    C. She is going to fight with the man.

27. A. She doesn't eat breakfast.
    B. Her mom prepares breakfast for her.
    C. She eats breakfast at a food stand.

28. A. A lunch box.
    B. Magazines and newspapers.

C. Some drinks.

29. A. She doesn't like singing.

B. She wants to know why the man is singing.

C. She will join them.

30. A. At the police station.

B. At the bakery.

C. At the post office.

第一部分：看圖辨義聽力詳述解答

(A) 1. For question 1, please look at picture A.

What is the girl probably saying to the boy?

A. Sorry! Does it hurt?

B. Where are you from?

C. It's none of your business.

【單字】hurt (v.) 受傷，(n.) 傷；痛

【句型】none of your business = no business of yours（沒你的事！別多管閒事！）

(A) 2. For question 2, please look at picture B.

What is on the desk?

A. 2 books.

B. 3 pencils.

C. 1 ball.

(A) 3. For question 3, please look at picture C.

How much is the fare for the bus to Kenting?

A. $ 350.

B. $ 500.

C. $ 200.

【單字】fare (n.) 車費

（A） 4. For question 4, please look at picture D.

Where are they?

A. They are in a KTV.

B. They are in an Internet Cafe.

C. They are in a library.

【單字】Internet Cafe (n.) 網咖

（A） 5. For question 5, please look at picture E.

Who wrote the letter?

A. Michelle Cart.

B. Charles Chen.

C. Los Angeles.

【英文常識】西式信封左上角為寄件人，右下角為收件人，且
住址由小（地方）而大（地方），與中式住址相反。

（B） 6. For question 6, please look at picture F.

What are they doing?

A. They are hugging.

B. They are shaking hands.

C. They are kissing.

【單字】hug (v.) 擁抱
【英文常識】shake hands（握手）。shake hands 指的是見面寒喧時的
　　　　　　禮貌式握手，不同於男女之間緊握的牽手（hold hands）。

(B) 7. For question 7, please look at picture G.

What is wrong with the girl that is entering the classroom?

A. She is the first one to arrive at the class.

B. She is late for class.

C. No one in class is watching her.

【解析】enter 之後不須 + into，enter 本身即是「進入」之
　　　　意，所以 go / get into = enter。

(B) 8. For question 8, please look at picture G again.

How does the girl look?

A. She looks very proud.

B. She looks very embarrassed.

C. She looks very satisfied.

【英文常識】proud (adj.) 驕傲的，在東方世界驕傲似乎為負
　　　　　　面之意較多，但此字有時為「引以為榮」的意思，所以
　　　　　　須視上下文去決定其正、負面意涵。
【單字】embarrassed (adj.) 尷尬的　　　satisfied (adj.) 滿意的

(B) 9. For question 9, please look at picture H.

Where is the woman at this moment?

A. She is on the train.

B. She is on the platform.

C. She is by the lake.

【解析】at this moment（在這個時刻）與 now 意義相近。

【單字】platform (n.) 月台

lake (n.) 湖泊

(B) 10. For question 10, please look at picture I.

According to the picture, what is true?

A. They are all very excited.

B. The policeman is going to give the girls a ticket.

C. The girls follow the traffic rules.

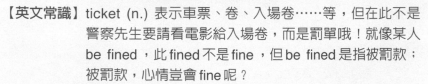

【片語】according to (prep.) 根據……

follow the traffic rules 遵守交通規則

【英文常識】ticket (n.) 表示車票、卷、入場卷……等，但在此不是
警察先生要請看電影給入場卷，而是罰單哦！就像某人
be fined，此 fined 不是 fine，但 be fined 是指被罰款；
被罰款，心情豈會 fine 呢？

第二部分：問答聽力詳述解答

(B) 11. How are you?

    A. I am 17 years old.

    B. I am fine. How about you?

    C. I am from Canada.

(A) 12. Today is really cold.

    A. It is, isn't it?

    B. Your dream will come true.

    C. Wow, it is so delicious.

(C) 13. Can I use your phone?

    A. Pretty good, and you?

    B. I am serious.

    C. Sure, go ahead.

【單字】serious (adj.) 嚴重的、嚴肅的

【片語】go ahead 請；請便

(C) 14. What does your father do?

    A. How do you do?

    B. He is not busy now.

    C. He is a dentist.

【單字】dentist (n.) 牙醫

(C) 15. Your last name, please.

    A. Yes, I won't be the last one.

    B. OK. I will know soon.

    C. Lin, L-I-N.

【英文常識】last name 為姓氏

          last name = family name = surname，而名字為 first name = given name，在西方名字放前，姓氏放後。

(C) 16. Would you like to go for lunch with me?

    A. Yes, I did.

    B. No, I am on vacation now.

    C. Thanks! I am not hungry at all.

【片語】on vacation 度假

(B) 17. May I help you, madam?

    A. I will help you with the homework later.

    B. Yes, I am looking for a necktie for my husband.

    C. No, I am going to help you.

名 師 解 析

【單字】necktie (n.) 領帶

(A) 18. Hello! May I talk to Jean?

　　　A. She is not home.

　　　B. Jean is my good friend.

　　　C. Let's have a talk.

(B) 19. How often does the bus come?

　　　A. For many years.

　　　B. Every 20 minutes.

　　　C. Come on! Let's go have fun.

 名 師 解 析

【片語】How often...? 多久一次？（指頻率）

　　　every 20 minutes 每隔 20 分鐘

　　　have fun = have a good time 指祝福對方玩得高興

　　　而 go and have fun，為相似的意思，其中 and 可以省略。

(C) 20. When will your father come back?

　　　A. Yes, he did.

　　　B. No, he won't.

　　　C. In a couple of hours.

【單字】couple (n.) 一對情人或一對夫妻，而 a couple of 在生
　　　活中表示二至三個之意。

第三部分：簡短對話聽力詳述解答

（C）21. **Man:** Why didn't you put any sugar in the coffee?

　　　Woman: I am too fat, and I need to go on a diet.

　　　Man: You are not fat at all.

　　　Question: What does the man mean?

　　　A. The woman really needs to be on a diet.

　　　B. The man wants the woman to lose some weight.

　　　C. The woman doesn't look fat.

【片語】go / be on a diet (v.) 節食
　　　lose weight (v.) 減肥

（B）22. **Woman:** What did you think of the movie, honey?

　　　Man: I was so tired that I fell asleep. I missed some
　　　　　part of it.

　　　Woman: I can't believe it. It was so touching.

　　　Question: According to the man, what is true about the
　　　　　movie?

　　　A. The movie was terrific.

B. He did not watch all of the movie.

C. He enjoyed the movie very much.

名師解析

【片語】fall asleep (v.) 睡著了，注意動詞三態— fall／fell／fallen

【單字】miss (v.) 錯過

touching (adj.) 感人的

terrific (adj.) 太棒了！

（B）23. **Woman:** Excuse me, when is the next express train to Kaohsiung?

Man: Not until three forty.

Woman: Oh, no! I need to wait for an hour.

Question: What time is it when the conversation takes place?

A. It's 4:30.

B. It's 2:40.

C. It's 3:40.

名師解析

【單字】express 當動詞意為表達，但 express 在此為形容詞「快捷的」，表快捷的郵政或運輸交通。

【解析】not until...，直到……才……，所以 Not until three forty 在此表示直到 3 點 40 分才有快捷火車去高雄。

（C）24. **Man:** Can I call you tomorrow morning?

Woman: You know I am a night owl. So can you call

me later?

Man: Then I will call you at noon tomorrow.

Question: According to the conversation, which is true?

A. The man will call the woman in the early morning.

B. The woman doesn't like the man.

C. The woman goes to bed late.

【單字】night owl (n.) 指晚睡的人，owl (n.) 為貓頭鷹。

go to bed late 指的是晚睡，晚睡千萬不可逐字譯成 sleep late，sleep late 指的是睡到很晚才起床，與 go to bed late 「晚睡」是完全不同的意思。

(C) 25. **Man:** Can you turn down the TV?

Woman: Why?

Man: I am studying now.

Question: What is the woman doing now?

A. She is sleeping.

B. She is studying.

C. She is watching TV.

【片語】turn down 可以是拒絕或關小聲，在此是關小聲之意。

turn up 開大聲

turn on 打開

turn off 關掉

（A）26. **Woman:** It is freezing cold today. Do you mind if I close the window?

Man: Of course not.

Question: What is the woman likely going to do next?

A. She is going to close the window.

B. She is going to open the window.

C. She is going to fight with the man.

【單字】freeze (v.) 冰凍，而 freezing cold 表示非常地冷 = very cold

【片語】fight with... 與⋯⋯打架或吵架。

【句型】當對方問 Do/Would you mind...你介意嗎？，而要表示願意配合時，即表「不介意」，回答就必須是 No 或 Of course not.

（C）27. **Man:** What do you usually have for breakfast?

Woman: You know my mom is a businesswoman. It is impossible for her to prepare breakfast for me. I go to a fast food stand before I go to school.

Man: I see. I eat breakfast at home.

Question: What does the woman mean?

A. She doesn't eat breakfast.

B. Her mom prepares breakfast for her.

C. She eats breakfast at a food stand.

【單字】fast food (n.) 快餐　　　stand (n.) 攤位

（C）28. **Woman:** Where have you been? We are all looking for you. The bus is going to leave!

Man: I was afraid you might be thirsty so I bought something for you. Here you are.

Woman: Oooh! How sweet you are!

Question: What did the man probably buy?

A. A lunch box.

B. Magazines and newspapers.

C. Some drinks.

【片語】look for...尋找……

【句型】Here you are.（你要的東西在這裏。）

（C）29. **Man:** Do you want to come with us to sing karaoke?

Woman: Why not?

Question: What does the woman mean?

A. She doesn't like singing.

B. She wants to know why the man is singing.

C. She will join them.

【單字】karaoke (n.) 卡拉 OK

join (v.) 參加、加入

【句型】Why not? 表示「為何不？當然好囉！」

(C) 30. **Man:** 10 five-dollar stamps, please.

Woman: Fifty dollars, please.

Man: Here you are.

Woman: Here are your stamps.

Question: Where did the conversation take place?

A. At the police station.

B. At the bakery.

C. At the post office.

【單字】10 five-dollar stamps 即「10張5元的郵票」

bakery (n.) 麵包店

模擬試題答案卡區

模擬試題答案卡區

模擬試題答案卡區

全民英檢解題攻略

曾利娟老師累積多年的教學經驗,加上赴美進修的心得,創造出獨特的圖像式單字記憶及圖像自然發音等法則。為了能夠幫助更多人,曾老師將各種背誦秘訣編輯成冊,毫不保留地公開所有技巧,讓同學們都能瞬間提昇英文能力。

只要記住曾老師所傳授的方法,不用死背,就能獲得英文大跳躍的武功秘笈!

圖像單字記憶法
定價250元

圖像自然發音法
定價180元

English Guide 101

全民英檢初級聽力測驗 (附MP3光碟)

著者	曾利娟（Melody）
責任編輯	劉宜珍
審校	Josh Myers 、謝欽仰
校稿	呂昱慧、廖怡惠
錄音	Laura Titus Heffer 、Aaron Bettinger
內頁繪圖	徐世昇

發行人	陳銘民
發行所	晨星出版有限公司
	台中市 407 工業區 30 路 1 號
	TEL:(04)23595820　FAX:(04)23597123
	E-mail:morning@morningstar.com.tw
	http://www.morningstar.com.tw
	行政院新聞局局版台業字第 2500 號
法律顧問	甘龍強 律師
印製	知文企業（股）公司　TEL:(04)23581803
初版	西元 2006 年 09 月 21 日

總經銷	知己圖書股份有限公司
	郵政劃撥：15060393
	〈台北公司〉台北市 106 羅斯福路二段 95 號 4F 之 3
	TEL:(02)23672044　FAX:(02)23635741
	〈台中公司〉台中市 407 工業區 30 路 1 號
	TEL:(04)23595819　FAX:(04)23597123

定價 290 元

（缺頁或破損的書，請寄回更換）

ISBN-13　978-986-177-046-8

ISBN-10　986-177-046-1

Published by Morning Star Publishing Inc.

Printed in Taiwan

版權所有·翻印必究

國家圖書館出版品預行編目資料

全民英檢初級聽力測驗／曾利娟著.－－初版.
－－臺中市：晨星，2006〔民 95〕
面； 公分.－－（English Guide ；101）

ISBN 978-986-177-046-8（平裝附 MP3 光碟片）

1.英國語言 - 問題集

805.189   95013226

請填妥後對折裝訂，直接投郵即可，免貼郵票。

廣告回函
台灣中區郵政管理局
登記證第267號
免貼郵票

407
台中市工業區30路1號

晨星出版有限公司

請沿虛線摺下裝訂，謝謝！

更方便的購書方式：

(1) 網站：http://www.morningstar.com.tw

(2) 郵政劃撥 帳號：15060393
戶名：知己圖書股份有限公司
請於通信欄中註明欲購買之書名及數量

(3) 電話訂購：如為大量團購可直接撥客服專線洽詢

◎ 如需詳細書目可上網查詢或來電索取。

◎ 客服專線：04-23595819#232 傳真：04-23597123

◎ 客戶信箱：service@morningstar.com.tw

◆讀者回函卡◆

讀者資料：

姓名：_____ 性別：□ 男 □ 女

生日：　　／　　／ 身分證字號：_____

地址：□□□_____

聯絡電話：_____（公司）_____（家中）

E-mail _____

職業：□ 學生　　　　□ 教師　　　　□ 內勤職員　　□ 家庭主婦
　　　□ SOHO族　　□ 企業主管　　□ 服務業　　　□ 製造業
　　　□ 醫藥護理　　□ 軍警　　　　□ 資訊業　　　□ 銷售業務
　　　□ 其他 _____

購買書名：_____

您從哪裡得知本書：□ 書店　　□ 報紙廣告　　□ 雜誌廣告　　□ 親友介紹

□ 海報　　　□ 廣播　　□ 其他：_____

您對本書評價：（請填代號 1. 非常滿意　2. 滿意　3. 尚可　4. 再改進）

封面設計_____ 版面編排_____ 內容_____ 文／譯筆_____

您的閱讀嗜好：

□ 哲學　　　　□ 心理學　　　□ 宗教　　　□ 自然生態　□ 流行趨勢　□ 醫療保健
□ 財經企管　　□ 史地　　　　□ 傳記　　　□ 文學　　　□ 散文　　　□ 原住民
□ 小說　　　　□ 親子叢書　　□ 休閒旅遊　□ 其他 _____

信用卡訂購單（要購書的讀者請填以下資料）

書　　　　名	數　量	金　額	書　　　　名	數　量	金　額

□ VISA　　　□ JCB　　　□萬事達卡　　□運通卡　　□聯合信用卡

• 卡號：_____ •信用卡有效期限：_____年_____月

• 信用卡背面簽名欄末三碼數字：_____

• 訂購總金額：_____ 元　•身分證字號：_____

• 持卡人簽名：_____（與信用卡簽名同）

• 訂購日期：_____年_____月_____日

填妥本單請直接郵寄回本社或傳真(04)23597123